Relentless Devil

SONS OF VALENTINO
BOOK ONE

KYLIE KENT

RELENTLESS DEVIL

KYLIE KENT

If you want early access to everything, yes
everything come and join my Patreon Group
Kylie Kent Patreon

Want to be involved in discussions and have access
to tons of give-aways? Join my readers group on
Facebook Kylie's Steam Room

Social Media:

Website & Newsletter: www.kyliekent.com
Facebook: @kyliekent2020
Instagram Follow: @author_kylie_kent_

Ebook ISBN 13: 978-1-922816-39-9

Paperback ISBN 13: 978-1-922816-48-1

Cover illustration by
Sammi Bee - Sammi Bee Designs

Editing services provided by
Kat Pagan – https://www.facebook.com/
PaganProofreading

This book contains scenes of sexual acts, profanity, and violence. If any of these are triggers for you, you should consider skipping this read.

This is a work of fiction. Names, characters, businesses, places, events, and incidents are either the products of the author's imagination or used in a fictitious manner. Any resemblance to actual persons, living or dead, or actual events is purely coincidental.

This book is dedicated to you. Thank you for wanting and loving a devilishly delicious mafia boss book boyfriend just as much I do!

Who knows? The next time you run into a cafe, you may just find your very own Theo. Never give up hope. After all, what's life without goals?

CHAPTER 1
Maddie

"Shit, shit, shit!" I run down the stairs and see the train leaving the platform. My train. The same one I had to be on if I wanted any chance of making it to work on time.

I sit down on the counter and wait the five minutes it takes for the next train to arrive. I jump on, my hope of getting a seat squashed the minute I step through the doors. Just like my body, as I squeeze my way inside and grab on to the metal bar. I spend the next forty minutes standing between a sweaty, overweight, middle-aged man and a hipster teen whose music is blaring so loud out of his headphones it's giving me a headache.

As soon as the train arrives at my stop, I push my way through the doors. I look at my watch—my crappy Walmart watch that is held together with an elastic band wrapped around it. It doesn't really matter though. Even if it were a fancy expensive timepiece, it'd still say the same thing.

I'm late.

"Fuck it," I mumble to myself, running back up the stairs. I'm just going to have to leg it. So what if I turn up covered in sweat? I need this job. I can't be late. Gripping the strap of my bag on my shoulder, I rush down the sidewalk, doing my best to avoid bumping into the herd of foot traffic.

Ten minutes later, while panting for breath, I finally see the finish line. Grind the Bean, the coffee shop in Midtown Manhattan where I work the morning shift. My afternoons are set aside for Lilah, my little sister, whenever she doesn't have treatment. She spends three days a week at the dialysis clinic. My best friend and sister from another mister, Gia, takes Lilah to all of her appointments, while my nights are spent working at a dive bar two blocks down from our crappy little apartment in Brooklyn.

If you asked me two years ago what I'd be doing at the ripe old age of twenty-one, it wouldn't have been being the sole caregiver to my fifteen-year-old sister. I never imagined that Lilah and I would be orphans. But here we are, and there's no use crying over the crappy cards we've been dealt. It won't bring my mom and dad back, and it won't heal my sister.

I just have to keep going, keep looking for a way to afford her treatment and find her a new kidney.

That last one I'll admit feels a little out of my control. It's not like I can just go and harvest an organ for her. Trust me, I've thought about it.

I run through the door and smack-bang into a wall. A solid wall of abs, pecs, and rippling muscles hidden under the softest of fabrics—which my fingertips are enjoying the feel of way too much. I remove my hands from the owner of said fabric and abs. That's when I see the coffee running down his outstretched arm.

"Shit, I'm so sorry." I look around. There are two men in dark suits behind him, both glaring at me. "Here, I can clean that for you. I'm sorry—oh! I'll make you a new cup. It won't take a moment." I grab his hand, like I have every right to touch this stranger, and drag him over to the bar area. "Sit here. I'll be right back." I walk around to the coffee machine.

Shit, what did he have?

Anna leans over my shoulder. "Tall black," she whispers the answer to my wordless question before adding, "You're late, again. I covered for you but Heath is on a warpath."

I make the coffee and wet a clean towel with warm water. Walking back over to Mr. Tall-Dark-and-Solid, I place the new takeaway cup on the counter. "Here, show me your arm." I hold out my hand and wait. The guy tilts his head and stares me down. He hasn't said a single word. For a minute, I think he's going to curse me out, yell at me for ruining his expensive suit or some shit, then he smiles and raises his arm. I dab the wet towel on the sleeve of his jacket, trying in vain to remove the coffee stain. "Shit, I'm so sorry," I say again.

His hand covers mine, stopping my frantic scrubbing motion. "It's fine. Trust me, bambolina, I've had substances far worse than coffee stain my clothing."

I'm so lost in the husky tone of his voice, the dark greenish-brown orbs of his eyes, that I don't hear Heath walk up behind me. AKA, the boss from Hell. "Maddie, you're late again. Don't think I'm not docking your pay for the hour," he grumbles.

I snatch my hand away from the gorgeous stranger and spin around. "An hour! I was only ten minutes late. You can't dock me an hour, Heath," I plead, knowing it's useless. The guy doesn't have a nice bone in his body.

"I can and I will. Take it or leave it. Now I suggest you get to work if you actually want to keep your job." Spittle flies out as he yells at me. And all other sound in the café dissipates to white noise.

My fists clench and I nod my head as I make my way to the back room. I will not give that egotistical, power-hungry bastard the pleasure of seeing my teary eyes. After I put my bag in my locker, I wet my face and wrap an apron around my waist.

I can do this. It's for Lilah. *No, I have to do this*. We need the money from this job. By the time I walk back out to the counter, everyone is going about their business as usual. I look to the spot where I left Mr. Tall-Dark-and-Solid and find it empty.

I take over for Anna at the cash register and plaster a big ol' fake smile on my face. "What can I get for you?" I ask the man standing in front of the line.

"Boss wanted me to give you this. Have a nice day." He hands over a folded piece of paper, turns around, and walks out.

Weird. I shove the note into the pocket of my apron and look to the next customer in line.

After the morning rush, we finally have some time to breathe. And as soon as we do, Anna pounces on me. "Do you even know who you spilled coffee on this morning?" She smirks.

"What are you talking about?" I ask, feigning ignorance. I know she's referencing the hunk in the expensive suit, but I'm not going to admit that his face has been popping up in my mind all day. Or that my hands have been itching to pull out the piece of paper from my pocket and read it.

What could he possibly have to say to me? Maybe it's the name and address of his dry cleaner's.

"Don't play dumb, Maddie. You're far too smart for that to work," Anna says. "You do know who Theo Valentino is, right? I mean, we should probably start brainstorming ways to get you a new identity, a ride out of town."

Theo Valentino. "Wait… Mr. Tall-Dark-and-Solid was Theo Valentino?" I might not be able to see it, but I'm sure my already fair complexion is whiter than Casper right now.

"Yep!" Anna pops her P.

"Why the hell didn't you say something? OMG, I spilled coffee on Theo Valentino. Great. Just great," I moan.

I don't know him personally, obviously. But I guarantee there isn't a soul in New York City—scratch that, probably the entire world—who doesn't know who Theo Valentino is. He's one of the most ruthless and feared mob bosses ever.

"Wait, that wasn't Theo Valentino. That guy was far too young." The infamous Don is much older. He has a wife, a family. I watch the news. I've seen pictures of him.

"That, my dear sweet innocent Maddie, was Theo Junior. His son. The underboss," she whispers, as though it's a big secret she's revealing.

"Whatever. It's not like I'll ever see him again. I'm sure he's forgotten about the little spilled coffee incident by now. You know, with how busy he must be, ruling the underground and all."

"Right." Anna rolls her eyes.

"I gotta run. See you tomorrow." I pivot on my heel and walk to the back room to grab my bag.

I spend my entire return trip to Brooklyn looking over my shoulder, feeling like someone's watching me. Following me. Yet every time I turn around, no one is there. It's not until I get home and pull my tips out of my bag that I finally pick up the note. My hands tremble as I unfold the paper.

A one hundred dollar bill drops to the table. What the hell? Who tips a barista a hundred dollars? Especially a barista who spilled coffee all over your thousand-dollar-plus suit.

Bambolina,
Thanks for the coffee. Until next time.
Theo

CHAPTER 2

Theo

Mousey brown hair, pale skin with a light dusting of freckles, and plain light-brown eyes. Nothing extraordinary. I should know. I've sampled supermodels from around the world. There's something about this coffee shop girl, though. I can't pinpoint it. But I can't get her face out of my head.

Maddie. When that fat fucker Heath was berating her for being fucking ten minutes late, I wanted to rip his fucking throat out. This woman, who is the opposite of everything I usually go for, had my dick harder than fucking granite the moment my eyes met hers. And for the fucking life of me, I don't understand why. All fucking morning, I've been trying to answer that question. Who the fuck is this girl? Maddie. That's all I've got. A first name, an image of her pouty lips, and a fucking hard-on that won't deflate.

My phone pings from the desk. Picking it up, I see a message from the soldier I had tracking her.

HUGO

Followed her to a shitty little building in Brooklyn, boss. Want me to stick around?

ME

No, send me the address.

Before I can talk myself out of it, I pick up my keys, lock my office, and turn to the two soldiers who usually tail my ass everywhere. "I need you to head over to the docks. Make sure that shipment we're expecting arrives in full." I don't wait for them to acknowledge the orders. I know they'll follow through without question.

It takes forty minutes to make the trip to Brooklyn. I'm sitting outside the apartment building Hugo's text directed me to, asking myself why the fuck I'm here. I'm about to drive off when I see her push her way through the door. She looks up and down the street. It's like she knows she's being watched. Jumping out of the car, I trail her movements, sticking to the shadows and remaining unseen.

Where are you going, bambolina?

Two blocks later, and she enters a shitty little

hole-in-the-wall. I really wouldn't have picked her as the type of girl to hang out in a dive bar. But what the fuck do I know? All I have is her fucking name and an address in Brooklyn. And she makes the worst fucking coffee I've ever tasted in my life. I took one sip of the cup she made to replace the one she spilled and spat it out onto the pavement. The rest went straight into the trash can.

I lean against the building and light up a smoke, drawing the poison into my lungs before blowing it out. "What the fuck are you doing here, Matteo?" I ask, without looking to where my younger brother now stands a few feet away.

"You know, one of these days your Spidey senses are going to go haywire and I will get the jump on you," he says, leaning against the wall.

"I think Mom taught you to dream too big," I tell him.

"What are you doing in Brooklyn and what the fuck did that bar ever do to you?"

"I want a drink. Come on." I walk across the street and enter the bar. It's dimly lit and full of hipster-looking college fuckwits, who think they're something they're clearly not. I find a booth towards the back of the room. Sitting down, I scan the interior until my eyes land on her. Behind the fucking bar. She works here? Why the fuck does she need to work two jobs? She's wearing a white singlet crop top with a little black denim skirt. Her shirt's so low-cut that every time she bends over the bar, every fucker in this place gets an eyeful of her cleavage.

Fuck me. Adjusting myself, I let my eyes roam up to her face. Bright-red pouty lips, pale skin, and those fucking unremarkable brown eyes that hold me fucking captive.

"You losing your touch, bro? Are you just gonna sit here and eye-fuck her from across the room? Or are you going to take her out back and fuck her so we can move on to the drinking part of the night already?" Matteo smirks at me. My fingers itch to reach out and slap that fucking smirk right off his face. But then again, he does have a point. I need to fuck this girl out of my system so I can stop fucking thinking about her already.

"Shut the fuck up," I tell him, pushing to my feet and walking up to the bar. The minute she looks over, I see the recognition in her eyes. Good, I made an impression on her too.

"What can I get you?" she asks.

I rest an elbow on the bar, crooking my finger at her so she moves closer. I can't help but look down her top as she leans towards me. "I want you to lose your panties and meet me in the bathroom in two minutes," I say, just loud enough for only her to hear me.

I should have anticipated it. I always anticipate when someone's going to strike. The slap she lands across my face though—yeah, I didn't see that one fucking coming. It shocks the hell out of me. I shift back, rub my cheek, and stare at her.

Her eyes are wide as she stares back at me. Then I see the anger that's quick to take over her features. "I'm not on the fucking menu, asshole. Now, if you want a drink, someone else can serve you." She storms off to the other side of the bar, leaving me standing there still staring after her.

What the fuck just happened? I order two beers from another server before reclaiming my seat opposite Matteo. "Not a fucking word," I groan at him.

"You *are* losing your touch. Fuck, never thought I'd see the day. What the fuck did you say to her anyway?" he asks.

"I know English isn't your second language. What is it exactly about the phrase *not a fucking word* that you don't understand?"

"Oh, I understand it. I just don't give a shit. This…" He points from me back to the bar. "Is way too fucking good to not talk about."

"It's not up for discussion." I down my beer and stand. "Come on, we've got work to do. More like *I've got something to fuck up.* Someone to fuck up. Anything to get the image of Maddie out of my fucking head.

Down at the docks, I find my distraction in the form of a fucking lowlife thief who thought they'd get away with stealing from me. He's currently chained up inside an empty shipping container, pleading for forgiveness. He might as well be pleading to a deaf man, though, because I don't fucking forgive. And anyone who thinks they can take what's mine doesn't deserve to be breathing the same fucking air.

"*A little off the top. No one will notice.* We must be giving off the impression we're a bunch of fucking idiots, Matteo. Fucking dicks who won't notice a whole fucking box of semi-automatics missing." I circle the sniveling bastard, like a predator circles his prey.

"Huh, well, I'm pretty sure I've been able to count since I was yay high." Matteo hovers his hand parallel with his knee. "And you, brother, I think you were born fucking counting."

"You're right. I love numbers. Ten, that's how many fingernails I'm going to rip off your greedy fat fucking fingers," I say, picking up the pliers, and count right through his screams. "Three." I tear his shirt open, retrieving the small knife that I have sheathed around my ankle. "That's how many seconds it'd take for me to jab the tip into the artery… right *here*." I drag the blade's edge over the side of his neck, running it along his carotid. "Five." Digging in a little, I slice the knife down the center of his abdomen, pressing just hard enough to cut through the skin, but not hard enough to cause too much damage. I'm not done with him just yet. "That's how many hours I plan on carrying out this little counting game of ours."

Matteo groans behind me. I ignore his obvious impatience and walk over to the counter containing my tools, inspecting each option while envisioning the sort of destruction they could inflict at my hands. Deciding to go with a piece of razor wire, I turn around and smirk.

"Ever had a digit removed with wire? I hear it's a good time. Well, not for the one losing the digit. But me? I don't feel a thing." As I'm approaching my target, the door to the container opens and my father walks in.

Without a word, Pops holds up a handgun and shoots the fucker in the head, effectively ending my game early. He returns his weapon to its holster and pivots to me. "Theo, get this mess cleaned up, then go and find your fucking brothers and make sure they're presentable enough for dinner tomorrow night." He points a finger at Matteo. "Your mother is expecting all of you there."

"Come on, Pops, I missed one dinner. One!" my brother is quick to argue.

"What have the Wonder Twins gotten themselves into now?" I ask him.

"It seems they like to think of themselves as little entrepreneurs. They've gone and set up a fucking cage-fighting enterprise over on campus," Pops says.

I can't help but laugh. That doesn't seem that bad. "What's the problem?" Sometimes I envy my younger brothers. They get to be whoever the fuck they want to be. Me... my life was planned out before I was even conceived. The first-born son. The heir. Next in line for the throne. Everything I've ever done has been to prepare me for my role. To follow in my father's footsteps. Don't get me wrong, I fucking want it. I idolize my old man. To follow in his foot-steps is a fucking honor. I just wish my younger brothers would appreciate the freedoms they're granted a little fucking more.

"The problem is that Luca is the fucking star fighter. One wrong fall, one wrong hit, and he's going to ruin his fucking career. Put a stop to it." My father doesn't wait for an answer. He walks out without looking back.

CHAPTER 3

Maddie

Opening the door as quietly as I can so I don't wake up Lilah, I tiptoe through the small living room, finding Gia asleep on the sofa.

"G, I'm home," I whisper. She groans before sitting upright. "How was she?" I ask. I honestly don't know what I'd do without Gia. She is my rock. How I got so lucky as to have a friend like her, I have no idea.

"She's good. Crashed out early." Gia stands and goes to put on her shoes. She lives just a block away with her mother.

"Can you stay?" I didn't have that feeling of being watched on the way home, but I'm still a little creeped out. Especially following my encounter at the bar with Mr. Tall-Dark-and-Douchey. *Yeah, I've updated his nickname after that bullshit pick-up line.*

Gia looks at me for a moment. "Sure, but I'm the big spoon," she says, dropping her shoes back down on the floor.

"Sounds good. I'm just going to have a quick shower." I escape into the bathroom before the questioning can start.

I was hoping she'd be passed out again by the time I entered my bedroom. No such luck. When I walk in, I find her sitting on the bed, scrolling on her phone. She looks up and puts her cell down on the table. "What happened?"

"Nothing happened. Can't I just want an old-fashioned sleepover with my best girl?"

"You can, but something happened. What happened? Is it Lilah? Did the doctors call?"

"No. It's not Lilah," I huff, plopping down beside her. "I slapped a mob boss across the face," I reply. *Really fast.*

Gia's mouth drops open. "Say again? Because I thought you just said you slapped a mob boss across the face."

"Well, I think he's a mob boss. That's what Anna said." I shrug. "He might just be an arrogant look-alike or something."

"Okay, I'm going to need you to start at the beginning. And don't leave out a single detail," she says. Once I tell her the whole story, she cracks up laughing.

"I'm glad my misery is so hilarious to you, G." I pout.

"Oh, come on, this could only happen to you, Maddie. What the hell were you thinking, slapping him? I mean, don't get me wrong, I want to track him down and tear his balls off. I won't, though, because I don't have a freaking death wish."

"OMG! What am I going to do?"

"Nothing," she says.

"What do you mean *nothing*?"

"Look, if he really is a mob boss and he wanted you dead, you'd probably already be thrown over the Brooklyn Bridge." She smirks. "Besides, he wants to fuck you not kill you."

"Shh." I hold a finger up to my mouth. "He can want all he likes. I am not now, nor ever, interested in getting mixed up with someone like him."

She picks up her cell and starts tapping away. "Oh yeah, you're so screwed." She laughs. Turning the phone around, she shoves the screen in my face. And I'm left staring at those dark, dangerous, sinfully hypnotic emerald-brown eyes.

"It takes more than a pretty face and a nice smile to get into my panties." I push her hand away.

"Oh, please, this guy? I'd let him harvest my organs to sell on the black market for one night in his bed."

Breathe in and out. I will not acknowledge the irrational jealousy that overcomes me at the thought of Gia rolling around in the sack with Mr. Tall-Dark-and-Dangerous.

"Seriously, you should have just met him in the bathroom. What would it hurt to get your rocks off anyway? Sex is the perfect medicine for stress relief, you know. I'm pretty sure that's in the medical books," Gia argues.

"G, he's a mobster. Dangerous with a capital D. I will not risk my sister's safety for an orgasm in a crappy bar bathroom." No matter how much I want those lips of his touching mine, or to feel his hands all over me. "Besides, it's not like I'm going to see him again," I add.

"Mmhmm." Gia doesn't say anything else on the topic.

Sunday's commute into Midtown is quieter than on the weekdays. It's early morning and I actually manage to score a seat on the train. I pull out my phone and do the one thing I shouldn't be doing. I Google Theo Valentino. When the search results come up with pages of news articles on the older model, I retype *Theo Valentino son*. Those keywords are a hit. On four different accounts.

How the hell do these people breed like this?

There are four sons. Theo and three others. All of whom look like they've just stepped off the Abercrombie catwalk. I wouldn't be surprised if these kids were developed in a lab. It can't be natural to be that good looking.

I read article after article on the great Theo Valentino, next in line to head their organization. Of course, it's all speculation and hearsay, theorizing what their family business entails. I put my phone away when my stop is approaching and try my hardest to shake that feeling of being watched again.

I arrive at Grind the Bean just five minutes late. Surely no one's noticed. I mean, it's only five minutes and it's a Sunday. My boss probably isn't even in yet. Walking through the door, I do my best to hide my involuntary groan when I see the man himself standing in my direct line of sight. "Maddie, good morning," Heath greets me.

I look around. There must be another Maddie somewhere, because there's no way he's talking to me in that overly friendly manner. Except, when I peer over my shoulder, there's no one behind me.

"Morning?" I say, although it comes out as more of a question than a statement. Rushing towards the back room, I drop my things in my locker and walk out, tying my apron around my waist. I pause when the little hairs on the back of my neck prickle. When I look up, I discover why.

It's *him*. He's here. Again.

Why is he here? I look over to Heath, who is purposely keeping his back to the counter. There are no other employees around at the moment. I don't have a choice but to serve him. I tentatively approach the cash register, plaster on a fake-ass smile, and say, "Good morning, what can I get for you?" I do my best not to make eye contact with him.

"Ah, coffee, black. Thanks," he replies.

I sigh in relief. He just wants coffee. That I can do. "Right, won't be a minute." I take my time making his order, trying to keep the tremble out of my hands. I've worked in this café for six months and I've never seen this man before. Now, he's here two days in a row. Why? Putting the lid on the cup, I place it down in front of him. That's when I make the mistake of looking up.

He tilts his head to the side and observes me. It feels like his gaze is searing straight through to my soul. I'm just hoping the world opens up and swallows me any moment now, because I'm stuck like a deer caught in the headlights. I know he's bad for me, but I can't for the life of me look away.

"You have no reason to be afraid, bambolina." He holds out a folded bill.

Taking the cash from his hand, I find my voice. "I'm not afraid of you, Mr. Valentino." I admit my reply sounded way more convincing in my head.

"It's Theo. Keep the change," he says and walks

out. Just like that. Just walks out. I unfold the bill and see Benjamin Franklin staring back at me. Again.

"**W**hat's wrong with you? You're more off with the fairies than usual," Lilah says. She's sprawled out next to me on the picnic blanket. The weather's nice, so we decided to make the most of it and come and hang out in the park.

"Nothing's wrong with me," I deny. It's not like I can tell my fifteen-year-old sister that I'm being haunted by the sinful eyes of a mob boss.

"Riiiiight," she says, drawing out the word.

"How are you feeling?" I ask, changing the subject.

"Fine." She stares off into the distance.

The little hairs on the back of my neck prickle. I look around and notice that we're not alone. I spot him standing on the other side of the small lake. Theo Valentino. If he thinks he's blending in out here, he's failing big time. The coffee two days in a row could have been a coincidence. The bar last night, not so much. Here right now, definitely not. He's following me. *Stalking me.* Whatever you want to call it.

I call it trouble. He's talking to someone beside him but staring directly at me. Two younger men approach him and he turns his head to them. They must be his brothers. That's when all four of them look over to where I'm sitting.

"Lilah, it's time to go," I say. I stand and start packing everything back into my bag. Taking my sister's hand, I hightail it out of the park and away from the scrutiny of the Valentino brothers.

CHAPTER 4

Theo

I wonder if I'll be babysitting my brothers for the rest of my life. I really would have thought going to college meant I'd stop having to bail the Wonder Twins out of trouble. Matteo and I have been getting those two out of all sorts of shit their entire lives. The twins are eight years younger than me and six years younger than Matteo. Though sometimes I feel like the age-gap between me and my siblings is much wider. That could be because they still act like they're in fucking prep school. Fucking idiots seem to find trouble every which way they fucking turn.

However, I must admit my heart did swell with fucking pride when Matteo and I crashed the little fight night they had going on. They've attracted quite the crowd—an Ivy League fucking crowd—full of trust fund brats, who have nothing better to do than spend Daddy's money on illegal bets.

The fact that Luca is undefeated is also a thing of pride. He's a fucking idiot, though, seeing as he's on track to go pro with his football career. Why he'd risk an injury he couldn't come back from, I have no idea. As soon as he won his fight last night, Matteo and I dragged both of their asses out of there. And I haven't let them out of my sight since. Hence why the idiots have been with me all fucking day. I could have dropped them off at our parents' estate. But they'd fucking leave and then I'd have to chase their asses down again, to ensure they made an appearance at Sunday dinner. They've both been missing a lot of dinners lately.

I told the two asshats to stay in the car when I stepped out. I don't know why I'm here. I don't know what it is about this woman that I can't seem to shake. But here I am, standing across a park, watching her eat lunch. She's sitting on a blanket with a younger girl. They laugh and conversate as they snack on a spread they have set out between them.

"Is that...? Holy shit, bro, what the fuck are you doing?" Matteo asks, stopping next to me.

"I told you I had to make a call."

"Yeah, you left this in the car. Thought you might need it." He waves my phone in front of my face. Fuck. This girl is inside my head so much I can't even lie about a fucking phone call. I snatch the device from his hands. "So, wanna tell me why you're stalking the girl from the bar?" Matteo asks.

"Nope." I could deny that I am in fact stalking her ass, but what's the fucking point?

"She's not your usual type," he comments as he eyes her from a distance.

"What's up with you two?" Romeo says as he and Luca stop just behind us.

"I thought I told you to wait in the car," I groan.

"You did, but I had to piss." Luca smirks.

"Theo here found the one woman in the whole of fucking New York City—fuck, probably the country —who won't fall at his feet." Matteo laughs, pointing in Maddie's direction.

"Seriously? You're getting old." Romeo screws up his face like he's in pain before turning to his twin. "Luc, just put me out of my misery if that ever fucking happens to me, man."

"Shut up. Let's go," I tell them as I watch Maddie pack up her little picnic in a hurry and walk off.

An hour later, I pull the car into the driveway of our parents' estate. None of us still live here, much to our mother's dismay. She's really not coping too well, being an empty nester. I walk in and find her in the kitchen. "Ma, how are you?" I ask, tugging her in for a hug and kissing her cheek.

"Better now that you're here. Did you bring your brothers?" she asks.

"Yep, all fucking three of them," I groan.

Mom beams. "Thank you. Dinner won't be much longer. Sit down. Tell me everything."

I grab a stool at the counter but I don't open my mouth. My mother always wants to know everything that I do—obviously, I don't tell her. "Do you ever regret meeting Dad? Have you ever wished you just met a normal guy with a normal job?" I ask her.

"No, never. I wouldn't change a single thing about our lives, Theo. Your father, you boys, are everything." She stops what she's doing and takes my hand. "Whoever she is, if she's the right one, it won't matter to her either." She picks up a stack of plates before handing them to me. "Here, set the table."

I grab the dinnerware and make my way into the dining room. We have staff for this, maids, cooks, etc. but my mother has always insisted they have Sundays off. Having set the plates on the table, I then head into my father's office. I find him sitting behind the huge-ass mahogany desk, grilling the Wonder Twins.

"Do you have any idea how fucking stupid the two of you are?" he yells at them. To their credit, they don't flinch. Anyone else would be pissing themselves right now. The twins turn to each other, sharing some weird-ass silent conversation between them.

"Well, if we knew how stupid we were, Pops, we

probably wouldn't be stupid, now would we?" Romeo says, ducking at the last minute to miss the stapler that flies towards his head.

"It stops now. There will be no more underground fighting empires in this family." He points to Luca. "And you will not get involved with any fights at all, you hear me. You're fucking lucky you can still throw at all after the bullet you took last year."

Luca was shot in his left shoulder at our cousin Lily's house. Some assholes looking to take out her new husband got into their home and started lighting the place up. My father's been pissed about Luca taking that bullet ever since. He can be a little over-protective at times.

"What do you think your mother is going to say if she finds out about this stunt of yours?" he asks, rubbing his temples.

"Wasn't planning on her finding out, Pops," Luca says. And I laugh. There is no way Mom won't hear about this. I wouldn't be surprised if she has every room in this house bugged, with the way she seems to always know everything.

"You really are fucking dimwits, aren't you? You still think you can hide shit from her? Well, it's your funeral."

"Come on, Pops, it was just a few fights. No one got hurt," Romeo argues.

"Tell that to the guys being wheeled out on gurneys." I slap him across the back of the head.

"Ah, what the fuck?" he grumbles.

"Do you two really think I have nothing better to do than come and bail your asses out of shit every other fucking day? Start smarting the fuck up." Walking over to the wet bar, I pour myself a glass of Scotch and down it in one go.

"Dinner's ready!" My mom's voice rings out through the intercom on the wall.

Great, I need to get this dinner over with so I can get out of here.

I almost make it through dinner when my father asks, "What's in Brooklyn, Theo? You've been traveling back and forth for the past two days."

Shit. "Have you got a tracker on me again, Pops?" I make a mental note to go over my car with a fucking fine-tooth comb.

"I don't need a tracker on your car to know your whereabouts, Theo." He smiles.

"It's a girl." Matteo laughs and then adds, "One who wants nothing to do with the likes of him." He points at me.

"Shut the fuck up," I growl, gripping the steak knife in my dominant hand.

"Stop, now!" Mom yells. "Matteo, leave your brother alone."

"What did I do? It's not my fault he's obsessed with someone who clearly isn't interested." Matteo shrugs.

"Who is she?" my father asks.

"She's no one," I say, scraping the chair along the floorboards and pushing to my feet. I throw the steak knife on the table and lean over to kiss my mother on the cheek. "Thanks for dinner, Ma." Pointing to Matteo, I add, "I hear Savvy's single these days. Maybe I'll go pay her a visit." I knew it before I said it. That I'd get the reaction I was looking for. Matteo jumps from his seat, and within seconds, he's swinging. I let his first punch connect, because I fucking deserve it for saying that shit to him.

After the first, though, I don't hold back. And before long, we're on the floor—Matteo pinned underneath me and the blows I'm delivering half-hearted. I don't want to fucking kill him, just use him as my punching bag to expel some of the pent-up fucking energy.

I'm pulled off him by my father. "You're done. Both of you."

"Seriously, you two are buying me a new vase," Mom says, looking at the shattered glass and scattered flowers that got knocked to the floor in our tumble. It's not the first time and probably won't be the last time we fight.

I hold out a hand to Matteo. He takes it and I pull him up to his feet. "Come on, I need a drink," I say, tapping him on the shoulder.

"You and me both," he agrees.

"Ah, stop right there. You boys aren't going

anywhere until you clean up this bloody mess," Mom yells.

I turn around, look at my brother, and smirk. "You know the Wonder Twins over there already offered to do it."

"What?" they say in unison, peering up from shoveling their mouths full of food.

I give them a pointed look, conveying my internal dialogue. *Do it or I'm telling Mom what you've both been up to.* It doesn't take them long to get the message.

"Sure, we got it," they both say at the same time.

Shaking off their fucking twin weirdness, I walk out with Matteo in tow. "Where are we going?" he asks.

I look over at him and smile. "Brooklyn," I answer, starting the car as he groans in response. "So, should we swing by and pick up Savvy?" I add with a laugh.

"Not fucking funny, Theo," Matteo grumbles.

"You know I'd never fucking touch her, man. She's like a little sister to me." I smirk, knowing that my brother definitely *doesn't* see his best friend since childhood as a *sister*. The fucker has been in love with her since before either of us knew what love was.

"I know. Doesn't matter. She's dating Dr. Jerk at the moment," he says.

"Who the fuck is Dr. Jerk?"

"Some asshole she met on Tinder. *Perfect teeth,*

perfect fucking job, perfect everything. If you ask Savvy," he mimics her voice.

"You know, if you actually made a claim, she'd stop dating all these losers," I tell him for what seems like the millionth time.

"She deserves better than what I can give her," he says, fully believing his own words.

"Maybe, but that doesn't mean you two aren't meant to be together." I really hope for his sake he pulls his head out of his ass. Sooner rather than later.

CHAPTER 5
Maddie

"**M**aybe you should just take him up on that offer of a quickie in the bathroom stall and be done with it," Gia suggests, after I've spent the last thirty minutes venting to her about my new stalker.

"He's stalking me, Gia. I mean, he turned up at the bar, at the coffee shop, at the park!" I wave my arms in the air. Exasperated. "He's dangerous. I should probably pack up Lilah and just go... somewhere, anywhere, as long as it's away from here."

"Don't be so dramatic, Maddie. I'm sure he's just besotted by all your charm. Maybe I'll come into Grind the Bean with you tomorrow—you know, get a feel for the vibes he's sending your way." She smiles.

"No. I gotta run. Thanks for being here, G. You're the best." I hug her tight. I really don't know what I'd do without her.

"I know I am." She swats my butt as I turn to leave.

I have to force myself to not run the two blocks to the bar, to not keep looking over my shoulder as the hair on the back of my neck prickles with awareness. Someone is watching me, again, and I have a pretty good idea who that *someone* is. However, every time I turn around, there's no one there. Or at least no one I can see. I imagine a man like Theo Valentino Junior knows how to stay in the shadows.

I breathe a sigh of relief as I walk through the doors of the crappy dive bar. Never in a million years would I have thought I'd be relieved to find myself in this shithole. Guess there really is a first time for everything. I head to the back, put my things away, and take my jacket off. Peering into the mirror, I reapply my red lips and fluff out my hair. The reflection staring back at me is not me. Instead, I see a girl who's way more confident with her body. Who is okay with using it to her advantage.

I could probably win an Oscar for the performance I put on here every night, pretending to be a completely different person. A person who lives life to the fullest. Always wearing that bright smile to greet the paying customers. Someone who will take shots with the sleazy slimeballs, or at least pretend to take shots with them.

On the inside, I'm dying a little more with every shift. I'd rather be home, curled up on the sofa with a book, or binging some trashy reality television show. I'd rather be helping Lilah with her homework. She's completing her high school diploma online. As much as she wants to go to school, I can't risk her getting sick, picking up some bug that will ultimately kill her. No, I can't lose her. She's the only family I have left.

Which is why I'm standing here in the first place. I tug at my singlet top, pulling it down to show just a tad bit more cleavage. "Whatever gets the tips," I mumble to myself.

The crisp one-hundred-dollar bills from Mr. Tall-Dark-and-*Obsessive* flash through my mind. If only he'd come into the coffee shop daily, I'd be able to get caught up on the rising medical bills in no time. But, no, I don't want him following me. I don't want him showing up everywhere I am. Like how he was standing there in the park today. Watching me.

I shake off all thoughts of Theo Valentino Junior and walk out to the bar area. I find Scotty behind the counter. "How're things?" I ask him with a bright smile.

"Better now that you're here, babe. How was your day?" he asks, wrapping an arm around my shoulder. I do my best not to immediately shrug free. He's a flirtatious slut, but a harmless one. Still, he really doesn't give up on his hope of getting me into his bed someday.

"Good. Took Lilah to the park for a picnic," I say,

stepping out from under his arm. "How's the crowd tonight?" I scan the bustling barroom interior, freezing when my gaze lands on a pair of furious greenish-brown eyes. Eyes that stare right through me. Crap. What the hell is he doing here?

"It's busy. Should be a good night," Scotty says, walking back over to his side of the counter. We usually split the bar in half, each serving our designated area. And tonight, my stalker seems to have seated himself in mine.

My skin heats up as I approach a couple of guys positioned in front of me. "What can I get you?" I ask, leaning over slightly, and smirk when both of their gazes fall to my chest.

"Two Jack and Cokes," one of them says, handing over a twenty.

"Sure." I flash my smile as I get two glasses and pour the drinks before passing them over the bar top. "Here you go." I move on to the next group of waiting customers and continue to ignore the dark shadow looming at the end of my section of the bar. This avoidance strategy works for approximately twenty minutes. Then it appears I don't have anyone else to serve. I guess I can't avoid him any longer.

I walk as slowly as possible, over to his end of the bar, and lean across the top, making eye contact with the man standing next to Theo. Judging by his looks, and my quick perusal of various news articles the other day, the guy's obviously one of the other three brothers. Continuing to ignore my stalker, I address the man next to him. "What can I get for you?" I offer a huge smile and shove my nervous energy as deep down as I can.

"Well, since I know you're off the menu, bella, I'll have whatever top-shelf Scotch you have stashed behind that counter of yours."

I pour a glass of McCallan and retrieve a cocktail menu. "Top shelf," I say, handing over the glass. I then place the menu on the bar top. Directly in front of Theo. "So you're not confused as to what's on the menu." I smirk, but make the mistake of looking up at him, and can't help the gasp that escapes my lips. "What the hell happened to your face?" I ask, reaching out to touch his cheek, only to snap my hand back before it makes contact.

What am I thinking? I can't touch him. I don't care if he's currently sporting a swollen right eye.

At least that's what I tell myself as I go about putting a scoop of ice cubes in a plastic bag. "Ice it," I demand, shoving the bag in his direction.

Theo's lips tilt up. He doesn't utter a word as he takes the ice from my hand. Energy zaps through my fingers as he slowly—and what I can only assume is *purposefully*—runs his fingertips along mine. "It's cute that you're worried about me, bambolina, but you don't have to be. You should see the other guy." He winks.

I look across at his counterpart. I can see bruises

forming on his face as well, and a cut runs along his left eyebrow. "I'm Matteo, the better-looking brother, obviously." He holds out a hand.

"*Obviously*. I'm Maddie." I laugh, placing my palm in his. Except he doesn't shake it. Instead, he brings my knuckles to his mouth. And just before his lips can make contact with my skin, my hand is yanked away.

"If you're lips go anywhere near her, I will fuck you up, Matteo," Theo growls.

The younger man laughs, holding his palms up in a gesture of surrender. I, on the other hand, do not find the situation funny at all.

"You can shove your caveman bullshit where the sun doesn't shine. I'm the only one who gets to dictate who touches me and where. Not you or anybody else. If I want to let any of the men in here kiss me, I will. And there's not a damn thing you can do about it," I yell at him.

His eyebrows draw down and his jaw tightens. "Just try to let any fucker in here kiss you, bambolina, and you'll be signing their fucking death warrants," he grits out between clenched teeth.

I laugh. "You can't be serious. You don't even know me. And I sure as hell don't know you. I think whatever ideas or fantasies you have playing out in that head of yours are just that—*fantasies*. This…" I point a finger between myself and him. "…is *never* going to happen." I make sure I put extra emphasis on the *never* part of that sentence.

Theo tilts his head to the side, observing me like he has numerous times before. As though I'm some sort of curiosity. His thumb brushes along his bottom lip, drawing my eyes to his mouth. A mouth that I bet would feel amazing against mine…

Nope, not thinking about that. That mouth will never touch me.

"Never say never, bambolina," he finally hums, as if just now reading my thoughts.

I shake my head and walk away, doing my best to ignore him for the rest of my shift. I know I should serve him and his brother more drinks as they sit there, watching me. I just can't bring myself to go over to that end of the bar.

If looks could kill, I think every guy in a ten-mile radius would be dead with the glare Theo's been sending out over the last few hours. Thankfully my shift is done. It's almost midnight and I'm beyond exhausted. All I want to do is curl up and go to sleep. I have to be up in just five hours to get into the city for my shift at Grind the Bean.

I say my goodbyes to Scotty and head out the

back. Grabbing my bag and jacket, I run into the bathroom and wipe off what's left of my eyeliner and lipstick. I don't like walking home at this time of night all made up. I've done it on occasion, and each time that I have, I've been mistaken for a working girl. It's much easier to go unnoticed without all the frills. I tie my hair up into a messy bun on top of my head and walk out the door. When I reenter the bar area, Theo and his brother are gone. Finally. Maybe he got the hint that I'm *so* not interested.

Or at least I won't allow myself to be.

CHAPTER 6

Theo

My patience is wearing fucking thin. I've sat here for hours, watching her ignore my presence. Watching her flirt with every other fucking guy in the place. I get that it's part of her job. But that doesn't make me want to pull my gun out and shoot a hole through each and every one of their fucking heads *any less*.

She can pretend I don't exist all she wants. I caught it though, the emotion in her eyes when she saw my face tonight. The fact that she went to the effort of getting me a bag of ice for my swollen eye but didn't even mention Matteo's obvious bruising. Which was far worse than mine.

I flick the cigarette I was inhaling to the ground and stub it out with my shoe. Leaning against the brick wall, I look up to the sky, expecting to see stars and end up seeing nothing. I fucking love looking up into the stars. You never really see them in the city though.

One of the best places for stargazing is Australia. My mom's sister lives with her husband in Sydney, and when we visit them, we often take trips out to the countryside. That's where you get an uninterrupted view of the stars.

I really should invest in a property upstate, where I can escape the fog of the city lights. I don't know what it is about the stars, but ever since I was a kid, I've been able to look up and get lost in them. I get the sense that there's something bigger out there than us. Something bigger than the life I was born into. The role I was assigned at birth. The door to the bar opens, and I immediately feel it when she steps out. The odd sensation I get every time she's near. It's like all my senses kick into overdrive, as I notice every little detail of her.

Her smell, sweet like a mixture of melon and coconut, wraps itself around me. Kicking off the wall, I follow two steps behind her. I'm not attempting to mask my presence tonight. I've followed her plenty of times over the last few days without her noticing me. Now, I want her to notice. Something about her fire and determination to turn me down is fucking appealing. I've never had a girl say no to me. So call me intrigued.

It's not just the challenge she's putting out though. It's more than that. It's the feeling I have in the pit of my gut that this girl is mine. I've never felt anything like it. My gut has never led me wrong before, so there's no way I'm about to ignore it now.

One thing I've always admired about my parents is their obvious love for each other. It's the kind of love Hollywood makes movies about. And I'm certain there's a book or two out there looking to share their love story with the world. It's almost fictional, yet the most real thing I've ever witnessed. I never thought I could have that. Never thought that kind of love would be in the cards for me. I'm always too busy. Looking after the business. Watching over my younger brothers. Too busy being the responsible one to ever relax enough to feel anything that resembles the contentment I imagine comes with falling in love.

Maybe Maddie is that love for me? Maybe I just want her because she said no. There's only one way to find out, and that's to not give up. No matter how much she fights me on it.

She quickly spins around, holding up an aerosol can, but before she can spray me, I take hold of her wrist and lower it. Wrapping my free arm around her waist, I whisper into her ear, "Bambolina, I know you don't really want to spray that shit at me." I feel her body relax as soon as she hears my voice. "I'm going to let you go, but I'll be keeping *this*." I take the can from her hand. "Just in case you get any ideas of actually using it." I release her and she steps back, her mouth gaped open as she stares at me. I take a peek at the can in my hand, expecting to see mace, but quickly realize I'm holding a bottle of deodorant. "What the fuck, Maddie? You were going to blind me with your antiperspirant? Why don't you have actual mace?" I hand the can of spray back to her, satisfied that it's not going to do shit to me.

"I don't usually have weird stalkers following me home," she says, spinning on her heels and walking a little faster.

I match her pace, strolling beside her. "Maybe I should be following you home more often, if you really think you can defend yourself with a can of antiperspirant?" I ask.

"It would have been worth trying," she mumbles, then looks over at me. "Why are you following me home, Theo? I thought I made it clear that I wasn't interested."

"You're interested. You just don't want to admit it for some reason. But it's okay. I'm a patient man, Maddie."

"Well, you're gonna need the patience of a damn saint, because you'll be waiting a lifetime," she says.

"Mmm, maybe. Maybe not. But I have a feeling it'll be worth the wait." We walk in silence for another block. I know we're getting close to her building. There's so much I want to know about her, so many questions I have running around in my mind. "Who was the girl you were with at the park today?"

As soon as I ask the question, her body tightens up, like she's getting ready for a fight. She folds her arms around herself, her eyes glass over, and she glares at me. "She is none of your goddamn business —*that's who she is*. I know you're obviously not used to taking no for an answer, but I need you to leave me alone." She dips her head down and then adds, "Please," so quietly I don't think she meant for me to hear it.

"You're right. I'm not used to taking no for an answer and I don't give up on going after something I want. But I won't ever cause you harm, bambolina. I can see the fear in your eyes. It's a look I've seen many times. A look I usually like seeing. But when I see it on you, it just pisses me the fuck off."

She doesn't say anything, and we walk the next block in complete silence. When we get to her building, I stop. As much as I want to barge my way into her life, into her fucking bed, I know that's not how I'm going to win this girl over.

"I'm sorry, Theo. I wish I could be the girl you think I am, or want me to be. But I'm not her. I'm the girl who works two jobs to make ends meet. I'm the girl with responsibilities beyond what any guy would want to take on. Trust me when I say this, it's best for both of us if you just leave me alone. Forget you ever bumped into me."

I reach up and tuck a loose strand of hair behind her ear. "The only problem with that, bambolina, is that you bumped into me, and you are not so easy to forget. I've tried," I tell her honestly.

"Well, try harder." She spins and runs up the steps of her building. I stand there and watch her silhouette until she's inside and I can't see her anymore.

An hour later, I'm finally pulling into my parking spot. I walk through my empty penthouse. The view of the New York city lights from the floor-to-ceiling windows usually gives me peace. It's almost like I can trick myself into believing I'm looking at the night sky.

Today, this whole place just feels fucking empty. I don't bother turning on any lights as I make my way to my bedroom. I strip off and step straight into the shower. I let the cold water wash over me before it heats up. Leaning my head back, I rest it against the tiles and close my eyes, breathing out a sigh of relief as my hand wraps around my rock-hard cock. It's been fucking begging for attention all night. Watching Maddie in that bar wearing practically nothing had my cock weeping for her.

I picture those red lips of hers as I tighten my grip, my strokes slow. Steady. I see her before me on her knees. Those wide eyes of hers shimmering with tears as she takes my whole cock down her throat. "Oh fuck!" I groan as my hand pumps up and down faster. "You will swallow every fucking drop," I grit out the promise of things to come as my seed coats the shower wall.

Fuck me. Maybe I should just dial up one of the hundred faceless names I have stored in my phone and fuck the thoughts of Maddie from my system. I know that won't work though. I don't think I'll ever get this girl out of my head. I jump straight into bed after showering, reaching under my pillow to make sure my gun is still there. My body relaxes into the mattress and I feel myself drift off with images of Maddie obsessing my mind.

The sound of footsteps coming down my hall wakes me. Within seconds, I have my hand wrapped around the metal grip, aiming the hot end of the barrel at my bedroom door.

"Theo, you here?" Luca's voice booms as he enters.

"What the fuck, Luc? Are you trying to get yourself fucking shot again?" I yell at him, slipping my sidearm into my nightstand drawer.

"Like you'd shoot your favorite brother." He smirks.

"Right now, I would. But he's not here," I retort.

"Ouch." Luca holds a hand to his chest, as though he's wounded. I get out of bed and walk to the closet. "Fuck, warn a guy you're naked next time, will ya? I don't need to be blinded by your junk," he groans.

"Don't barge into my fucking bedroom then." I slide on a pair of briefs and pull an Armani suit from a hanger. Once I'm dressed, I walk into the bathroom. "What are you doing here, Luca?" I ask when I notice he's still in my bedroom.

"Ah, I need you to talk some sense into Romeo," he says.

"Why? What's he done?"

"He's spending all his fucking time with this one chick on campus. Olivia, Livvy," he grunts.

"How the fuck is that my problem?" I counter as I run product through my hair. I don't have the energy to shave so I walk back out to the bedroom.

"It's not right. Something must be wrong with him," he says.

I stare at my little brother. The star quarterback of his college team. Surely he's not short on female attention. "Are you jealous? You not getting laid enough, Luc?" I ask him as I strap myself up for the day. Two guns slide into the holster on my chest while a third is tucked against one ankle with a knife concealed along the other.

"Fuck off. I get plenty of pussy. I mean, look at me." He waves a hand down his chest.

"Come on, I'll take you back to school," I say as I exit the room.

"Good. You can have a word with Romeo about how he's wasting his youth on this chick. I mean, she's not even his type," he rants from behind me.

"Luca, who the fuck Romeo wants to put his dick in is no concern of mine."

"What if I told you she's the daughter of Viktor Petrov?" he says.

I stop and spin around. "Is she?" I ask. Fuck, if that asshat has gone and got himself involved with a fucking Russian, I'll kill him myself. We may not be at war with the Petrov family, but we sure as hell will be if one of my idiot brothers sticks his dick in Viktor's daughter.

"No, she's not. Relax. Geez, you shoulda seen your face. You looked like Dad. So fucking scary." Luca shivers.

"Get in the fucking elevator. In the future, call before you drop in unannounced," I tell him.

"Why?" he asks.

"So I can make sure I'm not fucking home," I grunt.

CHAPTER 7

Maddie

"Will you stop fussing. I'm fine." Lilah swipes my hand away from her forehead.

"You're not fine. You're burning up. We need to go to the hospital," I tell her, already pulling my phone out to call Gia. She picks up almost immediately. "G, I need you to come get us. I have to take Lilah to the hospital. She has a fever," I get out before she can even say hello. I can hear the jingle of keys.

"I'm on my way. Meet me on the street," she says.

Hanging up, I slide the phone into the back pocket of my jeans. "Come on, Lilah, Gia's coming to get us."

"I don't need a hospital, Maddie. I just need to sleep it off. I don't even feel that bad," she grumbles.

"I'm not taking any chances. Let's go." I reach down and help her to her feet.

"I'm fine. I can walk," she huffs as I wrap my arm around her. She might be able to walk, but I can't let go of her. She's all I have in this world, the last of my family, and I need her. I need her to be okay. She doesn't argue any further as we walk down the stairs to the street. Gia pulls up to the curb just as we exit the building.

Opening the back door, I let Lilah get in first, then I jump in next to her. "Thanks for picking us up," I tell Gia.

"No thanks needed. You know I'm always going to be available when you ask." She smiles at us through the rearview mirror, or she tries to at least. I can see my own stress and worry reflected on her face. It's not long before we are pulling up to the emergency room doors. "You two go in. I'm going to look for a parking spot and then I'll come find you guys."

"Thank you."

I sit Lilah down in one of the plastic chairs before I approach the window. "My sister has kidney failure, she's on dialysis, and she has a fever of 104 right now," I blurt out to the nurse.

She looks behind me to my sister. "Bring her right through, dear."

"Thank you."

We don't have to wait long at all before Lilah is seen by the nurses and doctors. They ran a bunch of tests when we first arrived three hours ago, then gave her some medication that brought her fever down and something else to help her sleep.

Sitting here, watching her rest while appearing so sickly pale, I can't help the tears that fall down my cheeks. "I can't lose her, G," I whisper to Gia, who is now sitting on the opposite side of the hospital bed.

"You're not going to. They're going to find her a kidney any day now, and she's going to be back to that annoying, energetic, bratty little sister we used to hide from as kids."

I smile. It's wishful thinking. Even if they find a kidney in time and it works, I've looked up the cost for the medications and care she'll need afterwards. It's at least eighteen thousand dollars a year. We don't exactly have the best health insurance. I have money put away from my parents estate that will cover the cost of her transplant itself. But that's it. There's nothing else. All of the dialysis treatments, all of the medications, and everything else she needs right now—those bills I'm paying out of my own pocket. Or at least attempting to. I refuse to touch her transplant money on the off chance a kidney does become available. I will not let her miss out on a life-saving operation.

Somehow I will find a way to make things work. There is no other option.

The doctor finally comes back into the tiny exam room. "Maddie, everything looks good. She's got a run-of-the mill flu, so just keep up her fluids. I'm giving you a script for antibiotics, and make sure to give her some acetaminophen every four hours for the fever. But only for a day or so. We don't want to aggravate her renal system."

"That's it?" I sigh out a breath of relief.

"Yes, you can take her home when she's up."

"Thank you."

L ilah slept for three more hours. It's now just before five in the evening by the time we get home. "I can't thank you enough for today, G," I tell her as we both sit on the sofa, a glass of wine in hand.

"You never have to thank me, Maddie." She smiles. "I'm just glad it wasn't anything more serious."

"Yeah, me too."

"What time do you start tonight?" Gia picks up her phone.

"I'm calling in sick. I'm not leaving Lilah tonight. You don't have to stick around. You've been with us all day." I know I should go to work. And God knows we need the money. But with all the extra cash a certain Mr. Tall-Dark-and-Solid has been doling out this week in the form of excessive tipping, I can relax for one night.

"Like there is anywhere else I'd rather be," she says. "We're doing this right though. Pizza or Chinese?".

"Mmm, pizza," I decide with a smile.

"Great, you pick the movie. I'm ordering the pie," she says, tapping away on her phone.

Five hours later, we've gone through two bottles of wine—well, *I've* gone through two bottles of wine. Gia stopped at two glasses. After three rom-coms and a whole cheese pizza, we're both sprawled out on the sofa. "I'm so lucky to have you. I honestly would be so lost without you, G." My words slur slightly. I'm not drunk. A little buzzed, yes. But drunk, definitely not.

"I'm getting you a bottle of water. And I'll call my mom and let her know I'm staying over. Can't have you choking on your vomit in your sleep on me." She laughs.

"I'm not going to be sick. I'm not even drunk," I'm quick to counter.

"Yeah, okay, Miss I-Just-Drank-Two-Bottles-of-Moscato-on-My-Own."

"You helped!" I tell her with genuine shock. "Are you calling me a drunk, G? Because if you are, you might as well open that third bottle." I laugh.

"Nope, you need water, Mads." *Argh, I hate when she calls me Mads.* She knows it too. I don't bother answering her for that very reason.

There's a knock on the door. "Are you expecting someone?" I ask her, my eyebrows drawn down.

"It's your apartment, Maddie. Why would I be expecting someone?"

"I don't know. Maybe you dialed your latest booty call?" I offer in explanation. I mean, everyone I know is already in this apartment.

"Don't get up. I'll get it, princess." Gia glares at me still sprawled out on the sofa.

"Thanks, G. You're the best." I lean my head back and close my eyes. Enjoying the buzzed, relaxed feeling currently running through my veins.

"Where the fuck is she?" I hear from the front of the apartment. An irate gravelly voice. A voice that sends unwanted shivers through my body. Before I can sit up, a tall, dark figure looms over me. "Bambolina?" he questions.

"It's Maddie, actually, but you already know that because you're like a grade-A stalker." I laugh at my own joke.

"Are you drunk?" he asks me. He turns his glare to Gia before repeating the question. "Is she drunk?"

"A little." She shrugs. "It's been a rough day."

"I'm not drunk. Buzzed, but not drunk," I argue, not that either of them seems to hear me. "Why are you here?" I ask Theo. "And why would you let him in?" I ask Gia.

Gia smirks. "Well, I thought you might have dialed out for a booty call."

I hear a growl. An actual growl. Was that my stomach? It can't be. I'm so stuffed with pizza. "Again, why are you here?" I direct to Theo, ignoring Gia's remark.

"You weren't at the café this morning, and you weren't at the bar tonight," he answers.

"Maybe it's my day off. Guess you're not that good of a stalker, because if you were, you'd know that already."

"You called out sick, bambolina. Are you sick? You don't look sick."

"Maddie's fine. Lilah has the flu. We had to take her to the hospital," Gia's big mouth blurts out, and I glare at her.

"G, shut it. He doesn't need to know why I wasn't at work."

"Actually, I do," Theo says to me, and then turns that charming-ass smile on my friend. I see the minute she's hit by it, the Theo charm, and her whole body blushes. "Gia, is it? What's wrong with Lilah? And why did you have to take her to the hospital?"

Gia looks between us. "Ah, I think I'm just going to…." She disappears through Lilah's bedroom door.

I sit up and Theo squats down in front of me. Now face to face with my sour expression. "What happened to your sister?" he asks.

"How do you know she's my sister?" See? Not drunk. I can clearly remember I've never told him about Lilah or who she is.

"I'm assuming she's your sister, judging by the fact she's a younger version of you." He shrugs.

"Huh, usually people say Lilah is the prettier one. She inherited my mother's Italian complexion, while I inherited my father's pale skin." I shrug back.

"Your mother's Italian?" he asks.

"Yep."

"So what's wrong with your sister?"

"You really don't give up, do you?" I ask, tilting my head to the side. Part of me wants him to never give up, to chase me down until I can no longer deny that I want to climb on and ride him into the morning hours. Well, my body does at least. My mind, not so much.

"Nope."

"She has the flu, like Gia said."

"What else?"

"She has kidney failure. She's on the wait-list for a transplant. Not that it's any of your business." I yawn, a sudden bout of exhaustion sweeping over me.

"You're tired," he says, before he turns his head towards the bedroom and calls out, "Gia?" She appears seconds later, acting as if she wasn't eavesdropping. "What did the doctor say to do for Lilah?" He stands to peek his head into my sister's room. "Actually, don't worry, I'll get a second opinion."

"What?" Gia and I ask at the same time.

Theo ignores both of us as he puts his phone to

his ear and rattles off instructions in a fast string of Italian. I should tell him that I'm fluent. Lilah and I can also speak Russian. My parents wanted us to know both of their languages. I don't though—I don't tell him I understood everything he said. I know he just ordered a doctor to come here. I want to kick him out, argue that we don't need his help. But my desire to help my sister outweighs my pride right now. If he can get a second opinion, maybe we should.

He pockets his phone and looks over to me. "Bambolina, you need to put some clothes on," he deadpans. He's serious. I stand and fold my arms over my chest. His eyes dropping to my breasts with the action. And suddenly I remember I'm not wearing anything under the thin material of my shirt.

Shit. "I think you've forgotten this is my house, Theo. I'll wear whatever I want to wear."

He walks back over to me, and leaning down, he whispers into my ear, "You can wear whatever you want whenever you want. But I happen to like the doctor who's coming here right now. And it'd be a shame to have to kill him because you're choosing to look like... *that.*"

I gasp. He wouldn't kill him. "Wait... looking like what?" I ask, immediately offended.

"Like someone who's extremely turned on. I can see your nipples hardening through your shirt. I can see the flush of your skin." His hand comes up to my neck, his fingers gliding over my pulse. "I can see your pulse quicken, your breath hitch."

"It's the wine. I'm not turned on." *Deny, deny, deny.*

"Mhm, he'll be here in ten minutes. Your choice, bambolina," he says, stepping back, and I glare at him.

"Ah, Maddie, a word," Gia interrupts the stare down, before she grabs my arm and drags me into my bedroom.

CHAPTER 8
Theo

I watch Maddie stumble as her friend tugs her into another room. As much as I want to follow, I don't. Instead, I search through the kitchen cabinets until I find coffee. I set about turning the coffee pot on to make her a cup. It's shit coffee and I make a mental note to not only get her a new machine but also a stash of decent fucking beans. While waiting for the pot to brew, I send a text to Matteo, giving him a list of people to visit without me tonight. I won't be leaving this apartment until I absolutely have to.

By the time the coffee is made, Maddie is walking back out of the room. My eyes roam up and down her body. She's changed out of her pajama bottoms and the thin tee that I could see every inch of her perfect breasts through. Although I'm not sure the skintight jeans and oversized sweater that hangs off one of her shoulders is any better. Fuck, she's gorgeous in the most understated way I've ever seen.

I hold out the coffee cup to her. She doesn't say anything as she takes it and swallows down a sip. She also doesn't break eye contact with me. I'm not sure what she's looking for. What she thinks she might find. But I don't cower beneath her scrutiny.

Bring it on, bambolina. I'm un-fucking-breakable.

"Why are you here?" she asks finally, placing the cup on the counter. Her words are a lot clearer. Although her body sways a little. I reach out and grab hold of her wrist. That zing that has happened every time I've touched her runs right up my arm again. I lead her over to the sofa, slightly pushing down on her upper body to force her to take a seat.

I sit next to her. "I thought you were sick, or worse. So I came to check on you," I tell her honestly.

"Or worse?" she asks with a raised eyebrow.

I don't tell her the many worst-case scenarios that ran through my mind tonight when she didn't show up to the bar. In my world, the 'or worse' is not a nice fucking image to be stuck with. I lift a shoulder and shrug. "Doc should be here in five," I say instead.

"Look, it's not that I'm not thankful or anything. But *this*. It's not happening, Theo. I'm not letting some back-alley doctor anywhere near my sister."

I laugh. "Trust me, bambolina, Doc is the best there is. He graduated first in his class, at Harvard. He ain't no back-alley doctor."

She looks to the door that leads into her sister's bedroom but doesn't say anything. What the fuck do I have to do to get her on board with the realization that we, she and I, are fucking happening.

Leaning into her, I whisper, "You know, bambolina, as much as your mouth says you're not interested, I don't for one second believe you."

Her breath hitches and I pull back with a smirk. Without looking at me, she stands, a little more stable on her feet this time. "I need to check on Lilah. You can show yourself out, Theo."

It shouldn't turn me on as much as it does, hearing my name from her lips. I can't wait until she's fucking screaming it as she comes all over my cock.

Her friend Gia sits on the single seat opposite me. "What is it exactly that you want with Maddie? Because those two have been through a lot the last few years. If you're just here for a quick fuck, you're at the wrong place."

I send her a glare that makes most grown men whimper. Gia, however, doesn't budge. The girl's got balls. I'll give her that. However, I'm still not about to let anyone talk to me that way. Leaning my elbows on my thighs, I tilt my head as I choose my words carefully. "I'll let that bout of disrespect slip this once, because Maddie seems to be fond of you. But don't mistake me for someone who dishes out second chances like a stack of worthless flyers. I assure you

I'm not and I don't. As for what my intentions are with Maddie? That's none of your fucking business." I keep my voice quiet. Calm.

"Actually, it is my business. She's my best friend. I'm not scared of this whole mafia badass act you have going on either, so save your threats for someone who cares. If you hurt her, or if she gets hurt by getting mixed up in your fucked-up dodgy-ass world, I will come for you and no number of soldiers or high electric walls will save you," she seethes.

I smile. I like this girl. She's a loyal fucking friend. I'm glad Maddie has someone like that in her corner. Her confidence, however, is going to get her killed one day. I'm sure of it.

"What are you smiling at?" Gia asks.

"You're a good friend to her. I like that. Keep it that way." My phone dings with a message from Doc, saying he's arrived. I walk over to the front door and open it. The two soldiers who followed me here tonight stand on each side of the door—yes, I brought fucking soldiers. I didn't know what to expect. Like I said, I thought I could have been walking into something far grimmer. "One of you go and let the Doc up."

"Sure thing, boss," Anthony says as he runs down the steps. I don't shut the door. I stand on the threshold. Waiting.

"Everything okay, boss?" Marcus asks.

"It will be. Once the Doc is up, you two can head home for the night," I instruct. Marcus nods.

"Theo, you don't look like you're bleeding out?" Our family doctor greets me with a casual smile.

"Not me this time, Doc. Come in." I let him walk past me into the house before shutting the door. "Wait here." I enter Lilah's room. Maddie is sitting on the floor next to her bed. She turns her head to me, and the heartbroken look on her face almost has me falling to my knees. I don't care what I have to do. I will find a way to help her sister. To help her. Squatting down next to her, I whisper, "The doc is here. I'm going to need you to come and give him a rundown of what they told you at the hospital." I reach up and wipe away the tears falling onto her cheeks, not missing the way she leans into my touch.

Maddie takes a deep breath. "Okay," she says, and I pull her to her feet. I take hold of her hand, squeezing tighter when she attempts to tug it away.

I lead her back to the living room. "Doc, this is Maddie. Maddie, Doc," I introduce them.

Doc looks from me to Maddie, then to our joined hands. After clearing his throat, he nods his head to her. "Nice to meet you, Maddie."

"Thank you," she says quietly, eyeing the man with suspicion.

"Here, this is everything. Her whole history from the past few years." Gia holds up a folder full of papers.

"Ah, thanks." Doc takes the folder, then glances at Maddie. "Your friend here gave me a little rundown on Lilah. What happened today?"

"She woke up this morning with a fever, so we took her to the hospital. It's under control now, and they gave her some antibiotics for the next few days. We were concerned because she has kidney failure and is on the wait-list for a transplant," Maddie explains.

"Okay, how about I take a look?" the doc suggests. Maddie is hesitant at first but nods her head and turns to walk back into Lilah's room. I follow her, her hand still clasped firmly in mine. She hasn't tried to tug free of my hold again. I'm taking that as a win.

When she goes over to Lilah's bed, I release her hand as she leans over. "Lilah, wake up. There's a doctor here to check on you."

"Mmm, Mads, I don't need another doctor," Lilah grumbles.

"Too bad, he's already here. Just answer his questions and let him look you over. Please."

"Okay." Lilah sits up in her bed, finally taking in the room. She glances directly at me, and then at Doc. "Do I know you?" she asks.

"I'm Theo, a… friend of your sister's," I say. "This is Doc." I point to our family physician, who's busying himself opening his bag.

After twenty minutes of listening to the girls

answer questions about Lilah's medical history and current treatment plan, Doc packs up his bag. I escort him to the door before I address him again. "What can I do to fix her?" I ask in Italian.

"Besides finding a donor match somewhere, there really isn't much, Theo. It's a waiting game," he replies back in our native tongue.

I nod my head, unsatisfied with his answer. I shut the door, pull my phone out of my pocket, and call Matteo. "I need you to put some feelers out. I need a kidney. It has to be a match for the girl Doc just drew some samples from. Call him and ask how exactly we go about finding a match," I tell my brother. I stick to using Italian. Maddie and her friend don't need to be privy to these plans yet.

"Ah, any reason in particular, bro? That's a little strange, even for you," Matteo replies.

"It doesn't matter why. Just fucking get it done," I yell through the phone, frustrated with how helpless I'm feeling right now. Hanging up, I turn to see both Gia and Maddie staring at me.

"Gia, you should go home," Maddie says, not taking her eyes off me.

Her friend looks between us. "Are you sure?" she asks with a raised brow.

"Yep. I'll call you tomorrow."

Gia nods, picks up a bag from the small dining table, and sends me a warning glare as she walks out the door.

Neither Maddie nor I move, our stares locked. After a minute, she exhales a breath, "Whoever you just called, call them back and tell them to stop their search. As much as I want to find my sister a kidney, I'm not giving her one from the fucking black market."

I don't think I've ever been more shocked. "You understand Italian?" I ask, dumbfounded.

"Sí." She nods. "Speak it too."

"Shit. Okay." She doesn't want a kidney from the black market, fine. But I still intend on finding her one. Without taking my eyes off her, I dial my brother again. "Matteo, stop looking on the market for that kidney." I wait a moment and then add, "Instead, have every member of our organization pay a visit to Doc. Get everyone tested for a match." Not waiting for a reply, I hang up.

"That... Theo, you can't do that," Maddie says.

"I just did." I shrug.

"I don't even know what to say. If you think this, all of this, is going to get you a spot in my bed, it's not." She folds her arms over her chest.

"Bambolina, I'm going to find a way to help your sister. Not because I want to fuck you, but because I don't ever want to see that look of heartbreak on your face again." I walk up to her, cupping her cheeks with my hands. She tilts her head up to look at me. "Don't get me wrong, I do want that spot in your bed. That being said, I'd settle for the counter, the sofa, the table, the wall. Anywhere really. But I'm patient. I can wait." I lean in and kiss her forehead. "Get some sleep," I tell her, before forcing myself to turn around and walk out the door.

Each step I take is fucking harder than the last. I want to turn around and demand that she let me stay. Demand that she accepts that she and I *are* happening, whether she likes it or not. I'm not that kind of monster though. No matter how much I want to force her to submit, I need her to be a willing participant.

CHAPTER 9
Maddie

"Are you sure you're okay? I can take another day off," I tell Lilah. I don't know how exactly I'll swing another day without tips, but I'll figure it out. I always do.

"I'm fine. Go to work. I'll call you if I feel even the slightest bit sick again," she argues. She does look a lot better this morning. But I know her. I know she hates being fussed over. She hates feeling like a burden. Except she's not a burden to me. She's my whole world.

"Okay, but call. For anything. I gotta run. Love you," I yell out as I put my coat on and throw my bag over my shoulder.

"Love you too," she hollers back at me as I rush through the door. I'm going to be late. Again. I really don't want to know what Heath will have to say about it this time. I swear he gets grouchier and grouchier by the day. I've been working at Grind the Bean for six months, endured his grumpy ass for six months. My steps freeze as they land on the footpath in front of my building. Standing there, leaning against a black Range Rover, is none other than the man I'm trying my hardest to forget.

"Morning, bambolina." His smile is bright. And for some reason, an image of the Big Bad Wolf pops into my head. I bet he could charm anyone into thinking he's not who they think he is with that smile.

"Morning?" I question, my brows drawn down. "What are you doing here?"

"Get in. I'll drive you to work," he demands, opening the passenger side door.

"Ah, yeah, I think I'll take my chances on the subway," I say, pivoting to march down the sidewalk. Theo shuts the door, or more correctly he slams it, before uttering a string of Italian expletives. His steps fall in line with mine. "Why are you following me?"

"I'm escorting you to work. It would be a much more comfortable ride in the Rover, especially with the coffee I have waiting in the cup holders. But, if you insist on catching the subway, then we'll do the subway."

I stop and look at him. He's completely serious. He's going to follow me onto the freaking train. "Coffee? Why didn't you lead with that?" I turn around and stomp back to his car.

He opens the door with a smirk. "I'm not sure my ego can take the fact you're getting in my car with the promise of coffee, but refused with the promise of my company."

I bite down on my bottom lip to stop the laugh that wants to escape. "I think your ego is just fine. Besides, I happen to love coffee. I'm only just learning to tolerate your presence," I retort as I settle into the seat. With a shake of his head, he shuts me in and walks around the front of the car, looking up and down the street before slipping inside.

What the hell is he looking for?

"I didn't know how you like it so I got you a cappuccino." He gestures to the cup holder.

"Thank you," I say, taking the cup between my palms. The moan comes out involuntarily as the delicious creamy goodness hits my tongue.

"How's Lilah this morning?" Theo asks.

"She's better."

We travel in silence for another twenty minutes. It's not an awkward silence though; it's comfortable. Which is strange. I know I should not feel safe in his presence. I shouldn't even *be* in his presence. Yet here I am. In his car. Surrounded by his citrus, woodsy scent.

The growl of my stomach breaks through the quietude and has my face heating up in embarrassment. "Hungry?" Theo looks over at me and asks.

"I'm fine. I'll get something at work."

He shakes his head and pulls off the highway. Two minutes later, he's maneuvering through a McDonald's drive-through. He places an order for two breakfast sandwiches, handing one to me and unwrapping one for himself as he steers us back onto the highway.

"You really didn't need to buy my breakfast," I mumble around a mouthful of food.

"I'm not letting you go to work without eating, Maddie," he grunts.

"Okay, I'm not going to address that because I'm enjoying this sandwich too much, but let's put a pin in that statement and come back to it at a later date," I say.

I see his lips tip up at one side out of the corner of my eye. Somehow I get to work early instead of late. Theo double parks on the street, not showing a sign of care as the cars around us honk their horns. He gets out, walks around, and has my door open by the time I have my bag and all my trash from the sandwich and coffee in my hands.

"Thank you. For the ride and the breakfast," I say awkwardly. Because I don't know what else to do. He leans in and kisses my forehead just like he did last night. A part of me is disappointed his lips don't land on mine. But I also can't help but melt into how good it feels to have him kiss my forehead. I don't know what it is about the gesture but it makes me feel cherished in a way I haven't felt since my parents died.

"I'll see you later," he says, walking back around the car.

Entering the café, I see Heath looking at his watch and then me with a smile on his face. "Good morning, Maddie," he greets.

I look around. He's talking to me. In this nice tone. Again? Maybe he's impressed I'm on time for once. I really thought, after calling in sick yesterday, I'd be in for an earful this morning.

"Good morning," I say suspiciously, waiting for the other shoe to drop. Maybe Ashton Kutcher will jump out and tell me I'm being punked.

The morning has been busier than usual. I don't know if it's my overactive imagination, but I swear I've seen more muscled-up men in dark suits in the café than ever before. They're all *also* Italian. Which makes me think that either Theo is sending them in to check up on me, or they're all coming in to check out who they've been ordered to get a kidney donor test for.

I wish I had his phone number so I could text him to ask. But I don't. What would I say anyway if I did? *Hey, can you tell all your goons to stop coming into my place of work?* It's not like they've been anything other than perfect gentlemen. But it's still a little unnerving.

When my shift finally comes to an end, I half expect to run into Theo waiting for me outside. He's not there though. I'm midway up the block when an arm grips my elbow, turning me around. I bring my fist up ready to punch my would-be attacker. Except my wrist is caught midair. "Holy shit, Mads, that hurts." Matteo lets me go and shakes his hand out. "Who would've thought a girl the size of a peanut could pack such a punch?" He laughs.

"This is New York, Matteo. What do you expect to happen when you sneak up and grab a girl?" I ask.

"Most girls don't mind when I grab them." He smirks.

"Clearly, I'm not most girls." I don't really have time to deal with him right now. I need to get home. I need to check on Lilah. "Okay, well, nice seeing you. I don't mean to be rude but I need to go. Things to do, people to see, and all of that."

"Oh, I'm here to be your Uber. Come on, I'm parked down this way. Sorry I was late. Traffic was a bitch."

"I didn't call for an Uber," I tell him, though I'm not sure why, considering I know he's not an actual Uber.

"Theo got held up in a meeting and told me to come and pick you up."

I roll my eyes. That man really needs to get a grip

on reality. The reality that I'm not his property. I'm not his girlfriend, or someone he needs to arrange drivers for. I'm not really sure we're even friends. I don't know the guy. "Can I borrow your phone? Mine's dead," I lie, holding my palm out expectantly.

"Sure." After unlocking his screen, he hands his cell over to me.

I open his contacts list, find one number at the top labelled *boss,* and having heard him use the reference on Theo more than once at the bar, I dial it. The phone rings a couple of times before the call connects. "Theo, I don't know who the fuck you think you are, but you need to stop. This is taking the whole stalker thing to a new level. Surely you have better things to do than send your people to follow me around. Why is Matteo here to drive me home? I'll have you know I've been finding my own way home for years. Years, Theo. I don't need you interfering with my life. I don't need your kind of complication right now, and I certainly don't need to be distracted by everything that is... *you.* Sure, you're hot as shit," I ramble on, "sweet in a weird, stalkerish way, and you make me want things that I shouldn't want. But I don't have time for your crap. Stop. Tell your brother I don't need a ride home. That I'm more than capable of getting on the subway, which is what I'm doing right now." Finishing my rant, I hand the phone back before Theo can get a word in.

Matteo looks down at the screen. His eyes widen

and his lips tip up as he brings the device to his ear. "Ah, Pops, clearly that message was for the *other* Theo." He puts extra emphasis on the adjective as he looks at me with laughter in his eyes. "Oh, who was that? That was your future daughter-in-law I'm guessing. Clearly Theo has his work cut out for him with this one, but I have faith. He is a Valentino after all."

I'm frozen to the spot. I'm not an idiot. I know who I just cursed out. The head of the Valentino crime family. For some reason, I seem to let my guard down when I'm around Theo. And, apparently, it seems Matteo too. I need to constantly remind myself what these men are capable of. What they do for a living.

"Sure thing. Catch you later. Okay, I'll tell her." He hangs up the phone. "Pops wants you to attend Sunday dinner this weekend." He laughs.

"W-What?"

"Dinner. Sunday. Look, you can say no but is that really the first impression you want to make on your future in-laws?"

"I need to go home," I say in response.

"Your chariot awaits." He waves an arm out in the direction of his car.

As if too numb to do anything else, I walk that way and get in. Matteo rambles on as we make the trip to Brooklyn. I answer some of his questions with short responses, but for the most part, I'm stuck in my own thoughts.

What the hell have I gotten myself into? What the hell has Theo gotten me into?

"See you later, Maddie. Don't forget Sunday, although I'm sure Theo is more than aware of that invite by now." Matteo laughs.

I nod and walk into the building. Entering the apartment, I find Lilah sitting at the table with her laptop open and books everywhere. One thing I've always been thankful for is her eagerness for school-work. I know a lot of teens in her situation would have given up on the mundane task, would just let it slide. Not Lilah though. She's a straight-A student. No matter how many days she's been stuck in bed too sick to move, she always finds a way to get back on top of her studies.

I admire her strength like nothing else. Right now, I could use a little bit of that strength. "How are you feeling?" I ask her.

"A lot better," she says, looking up from her screen.

"That's good." I take my jacket off and make my way over to the thermostat, turning the heat up. It's freezing in here. We're at the end of November, and winter has well and truly made an appearance.

"Soooo, are we going to talk about that hot guy who was here last night?"

"The doctor?" I ask, playing dumb. Although it's not a lie. The doctor was a good-looking man.

"Nope, not him. The other one… Theo?"

"Ah, I'm going to hop in the shower. I need a nap before my shift tonight."

CHAPTER 10
Theo

"Theo, care to tell me why I just had my ear chewed off by a girl named Maddie?" my father asks me after he hangs up the phone and places it on his desk. Before answering him, I check my cell. Matteo should be with Maddie. I send him a message.

ME:

Did you pick her up?

MATTEO:

Yep.

"Theo, I have a lot of shit to do today. Why are you bothering this girl?" Pops is shuffling papers around on his desk.

"I'm not bothering her. She's a friend," I say.

"It didn't seem to me like she was keen on your

friendship. I think the word she used to describe you was… *stalker*. I didn't raise you boys to mistreat or scare women, Theo."

"I'm not fucking mistreating her," I growl, annoyed that he would even think me capable. "She's just still getting used to the idea of me—that's all."

"Well, Sunday dinner shouldn't be awkward at all, should it then?"

"She's not coming to Sunday dinner," I deny. I heard him mentioned that he expects someone at Sunday dinner. I just didn't know he was talking about my Maddie.

Fucking Matteo. Why the fuck would he let her call Pops?

"Yes, she is. I already invited her." In other words, he demanded her presence. Nobody ever says no to my father. Well, nobody other than my mother.

"She has to work. She also looks after her younger sister," I say in her defense. Fuck, I'm trying to win the girl over. I don't need her meeting my messed-up fucking family before I've had the chance to make her fall for me.

Fall for me. Holy fucking shit. Since when have I ever wanted a girl to fall for me? I've had plenty of girls claim to be in love with me. They were more than likely in love with what I could offer them, rather than me as a person. Maddie knows who I am. She knows I could give her anything, yet she asks for nothing. Acts like she doesn't want fuck-all to do with me. I know she does though. I know she'll come around, eventually.

"She can bring her sister with her," my father says. Subject closed.

"Fine. Are we done here?" I nod to the stack of papers on the desk. We've been running through reports for several of our legitimate businesses all day.

"For now."

"See you later, Pops," I reply before walking out the door. I manage to get out of the house unseen. As soon as I get into my car, I call my brother. "Did you drop her home?" I ask him first.

"Delivered safe and sound, boss." He laughs.

"Why the fuck did you let her call Pops?" I hiss into the Bluetooth receiver.

"Firstly, I don't think anyone lets that girl do anything," he says, and I can't help the smile that spreads across my face with the feeling of pride that Maddie isn't afraid to speak her mind. "Second, I didn't know who she was calling. She just asked to borrow my phone. She was obviously trying to call you, idiot. Maybe you should try giving her your number and then she wouldn't be calling up the wrong Theo Valentino."

"Fuck! Pops wants her at Sunday dinner," I groan, running a hand down my face.

"I heard."

"I gotta go. Catch ya later." I'm fucking dead tired. After leaving Maddie's last night, then driving back into the city, I think I managed three hours sleep before my alarm went off, so I could be back in Brooklyn to give her a ride to work.

I 'm startled awake by my phone vibrating on the bedside table. I swipe it up and answer without looking at who's calling. "Hello."

"Theo? Did I wake you?" An Australian accent comes through the other end of the line.

"Yes, you fucking did," I groan. "What do you want, Alex?" I ask my cousin's husband. When I first met Alex, I wanted to put a fucking hole through his head. In my eyes, no one is good enough for my little cousins. Hope and Lily. They're twins and look just like our mothers, who are also fucking twins.

I swear my family's cursed with twins. I just hope like fuck that curse skips me. Don't get me wrong, I love kids. I want kids. But two of them at the same time... yeah, I'll pass. I remember when Luca and Romeo were little. I remember how much trouble they got into together. Shit, they still fucking do.

"Lily wants to make sure you're all going to make

it for Christmas," he says in a tone that means: *you will fucking make it for Christmas and not upset my wife.*

"That's the plan." My brain is already thinking of excuses for how I can get out of it. I'd rather stay here, stay near Maddie. I could take her with me, but fuck, that would mean introducing her to my extended family and she sure as shit is not ready for that.

"Is something on your mind?" Alex asks. *The intuitive fucker that he is.*

"Nothing you can help with," I reply. Over the last year, he has become one of my closest friends, even if we are separated by an ocean. I found out he married my cousin after the fact. To say I was not his biggest fan to begin with would be saying the least. He loves her though. That much is clear to anyone with a pair of eyes. There is nothing he wouldn't do for her. Once I accepted that he is who she chose for herself, I let go of the hatred (mostly) and we've built a legitimate friendship.

Having the extra connection to the Sydney under-world, seeing as Alex is currently the king of that city, is just an added bonus. However, I'd still put a bullet through his head if he ever hurts Lily. Friend or not, nothing comes before family.

"Okay, well, I'll see you in a few weeks."

"Looking forward to it," I say, my voice dripping with sarcasm. I hang up and look at the time. It's fucking eleven p.m. I can't believe I slept this fucking long.

I send a text to Anthony, the soldier I have following Maddie tonight.

> ME:
> Where is she?

His response comes in immediately.

> ANTHONY:
> Still at the bar.

> ME:
> Any trouble?

> ANTHONY:
> None.

> ME:
> Follow her home. Make sure she gets in safe.

> ANTHONY:
> No problem, boss.

I toss the phone back down after setting my alarm for four a.m. I might not make it to Brooklyn tonight before she finishes her shift at the bar, but I'll be there bright and early to pick her up before she starts at the café.

I stop in at a small coffee shop and grab two coffees and a breakfast muffin for Maddie. Pulling up in front of her building, I stand there in the freezing-cold, waiting for her to come out. My fingers are almost numb by the time she walks out of the building, her glare directed at me. "Is this going to be a regular thing? Finding you out here in the mornings?" she asks.

"I can't promise I'll be here every day, but I can make sure someone is." I shrug, opening the passenger door. She doesn't argue as she gets into the car this time. Small wins. I'll take whatever I can get. "How was your day yesterday?" I ask her, handing her a coffee cup and the bag with the muffin in it.

She takes the cup and peeks inside the bag. "Uneventful," she says.

"Huh, I heard you made an interesting phone call." I smile.

"Really? Well, I don't know where you heard that, but there was nothing interesting about any phone call I made yesterday. Mortifying, embarrassing, yes. But interesting, no."

"You've sparked my father's interest. Not many people do," I tell her.

"I'm not sure that's a good thing, Theo. I don't know if you're aware of this, but your father is *the* boss of the Valentino crime family. It's probably best if I stay off his radar."

"He's a good man, Maddie. Most of what you hear on the news is bullshit." It's not really, but I have the best poker face.

"That would be more convincing if you actually believed it," she says, laughing.

Okay, I guess my poker face needs some work. "He wants you and Lilah to come to Sunday dinner."

"Yeah, I'm not bringing my little sister into the lion's den, Theo."

"Do you honestly think I'd ever let anything happen to you or her?"

"Well, here's the thing… I don't really know you, do I? I mean, I know of you. I know of your reputation, but I don't know you."

"What better way to get to know me than coming to have dinner with me."

"And your family," she argues.

"Yep." Before she can make up another excuse, my phone rings and my mom's name pops up on the screen. "Ma, good morning," I answer.

"Theo, why am I the last to hear about Maddie?" she says.

"You do know it's five in the morning, right? Can this wait?" I ask, looking over at the girl in question, who is staring at me with wide eyes. I reach over and grab her hand, entwining my fingers with hers. She doesn't try to pull away. *Again, small wins.*

"No, it can't wait. If you've gone and fallen in love with a girl, I should have been the first to know. Well, actually, maybe the girl should be the first but I come in a strong second. But, no, I find out from your father when he casually mentions there will be two extra guests for dinner on Sunday. Wait... Does she know, Theo?"

"Does who know what?" I ask her, confused.

"Does Maddie know that you're in love with her?"

"Ah, Ma, I gotta go. Talk later." I hang up, knowing full well I'm going to get a lecture about it later. "I'm sorry. My mom can be a little dramatic. Ignore her."

"Mhmm." Maddie looks like she's seen a ghost. She's pale.

"What's wrong?" I ask her.

"Nothing," she says and opens the bag. "This muffin looks delicious. Thank you." I'm forced to let go of her hand so she can eat her breakfast. We both ignore the elephant in the car: the fact that my own mother outed my feelings for this girl before I could tell her.

I drop Maddie off at work with the promise of picking her up when she finishes. She doesn't argue, doesn't say anything, as I lean in and kiss her forehead. Would I much rather be kissing her lips? Fuck yes. And I would if I didn't think she'd slap me for it.

I watch her enter the café before I get back in my car and drive off. Fuck. I don't know if I am in love with her like my mother insists, but there is something about her that I can't seem to shake. I've never been in love before, so how the fuck am I supposed to know what it feels like? I do know Matteo is in love with his best friend Savvy, and has been since forever. He's just not prepared to do anything about it.

I end up driving to his apartment. If anyone can help me figure out these feelings, it's my brother.

CHAPTER 11

Maddie

It's been four days, and each morning Theo has been waiting to pick me up. Two of the nights he came and sat at the bar while I worked. He didn't look like he wanted to be there one bit. Today is Sunday. I've been debating whether or not I'm going to accept his father's dinner invitation. I think if I don't show up I might be the first person to say no to the mob boss.

"What's wrong?" Lilah asks from the other side of the table. I'm off for the day so I made us breakfast: bacon, eggs, toast, and sausages.

"Nothing," I answer.

"Don't lie to me, Maddie. We promised." She reminds me of our pact to never, ever lie to each other about anything. Big or small.

"Theo's parents invited us over for dinner tonight," I tell her.

"And why is that making you stressed?"

"Because of what his family does for a living—who they are," I huff out.

"I Googled him, you know. I know who he is."

"So you see why going to his family's home for dinner is a bad idea, right?"

"Nope. I don't think it matters what they do, as much as how he treats you. Is he kind to you? Because he looks it to me, the few times I've seen him waiting for you in the morning," she says, shocking me.

"How?" I've purposely not told her much about Theo.

"The windows." She shrugs.

"Right."

"So, is he nice to you?"

I think of how he takes the forty minute trip from the city to Brooklyn each morning just to drive me to work. I think of how he always has coffee and breakfast waiting for me. I think of how he's taken to holding my hand as he drives. He hasn't pushed for anything more, though, and I appreciate him for that. That doesn't mean I'm ready to meet his family. I haven't even kissed the guy and he wants to take me home to meet his mother.

"He's nice," I answer Lilah.

"Well, I don't know about you, but I'm up for a home-cooked meal that actually tastes good." She laughs. Neither of us can cook anything very well, despite our mother's best attempts at teaching us. That thought has me wondering what my parents would think of Theo. Would they approve? My dad wouldn't but then again, he wouldn't approve of any guy. I do feel like Theo would be someone my mom would have liked.

"I'm not sure. I don't want to lead Theo into believing whatever is happening between us is going anywhere other than maybe a friendship."

"Why not? He's hot as hell." Lilah grins.

"Lilah! He's like fourteen years older than you. God, he's eight years older than me."

"Doesn't mean he ain't a looker. Come on, Maddie, you deserve to at least have some fun."

There's a knock at the door. "Expecting some-one?" I ask her. She shakes her head. I open the door to find the man in question standing there with a tray of takeaway coffee cups and a box of donuts. "Uh, hi?" I question.

"Bambolina, how are you?" He leans in, kissing my cheek.

"Um, good?" Again, my words come out like a damn question.

Theo laughs. "Are you going to invite me in?"

"Do I have a choice?" I fold my arms over my chest.

"Hey, Theo, it's good to see you again. Come on in," Lilah says from her spot at the dining table.

Theo smirks my way before stepping around me.

"Lilah, how are you feeling, sweetheart?" he asks her, placing the coffees and donuts on the table.

"Good, you?" She smiles at him.

"Can't complain."

"Why are you here, Theo?" Don't get me wrong, I appreciate the amazing coffee he keeps bringing. But really, it's been every day this week. Doesn't he have a criminal empire to run or something?

"It's Sunday. You two are coming to dinner tonight," he says, as though that's an explanation.

"It's eight o'clock in the morning. Do your parents eat dinner this early?"

"No, we're not expected until six. But I thought we could spend the day together. I have plans."

"I can't go out today. I'm hanging out with my sister today," I tell him.

"Lilah's coming with us."

"Lilah is right here." She laughs. "What are we doing, Theo? I'm going to run and get dressed now."

"Wear something comfortable—and warm," he adds. "Bambolina, trust me, it'll be fun." He gives me that trademark smirk of his. The one that has my panties wet within seconds. Damn it. What the hell is wrong with me? Why can't I say no to this guy?

"We can't be out in the cold for long periods of time. I can't risk Lilah getting sick." I don't add the part about how I'm still trying to find a way to pay off the bill from the last emergency room visit.

"We won't be. I'll make sure of it," he says.

"Okay, wait here. Don't touch anything," I tell him as I close myself inside my bedroom. I pick up my phone and send a text message to Gia.

ME:

Lilah and I are spending the day with Theo. He has plans apparently. If we go missing, hunt him down and make it hurt!!!

I add some little knife emojis at the end.

GIA:

Don't be dramatic. That boy is smitten with you, Maddie. As if anything is going to happen.

I'm reminded of his mother's words when she called him a few days ago. She said he was in love. Something neither of us has brought up again. He can't be in love with me; he doesn't know me.

Butterflies swarm my stomach as I dig through my closet for something to wear. Why do I even care? I'm trying to get him to pay me less attention, aren't I? Deciding on a pair of black jeans and a white sweater, I pair it with some black ankle boots and a grey coat. I brush my hair out quickly before wrapping a scarf around my neck. By the time I walk out, my sister is chatting up a storm with Theo while shoving her face with a donut.

"Lilah, you're going to need gloves and a scarf," I

tell her. She scoffs but heads into her room to retrieve the items.

"You look beautiful, bambolina," Theo says.

"No, I don't." I peer down at the very casual outfit I put together.

"You could be wearing a potato sack and I'd still think you were the most beautiful creature in the room."

I'm saved from answering *that* when Lilah comes out. "Okay, let's do this." She beams, full of excitement. It makes me happy to see her so enthusiastic about something. I let Theo take my hand as he leads us out of the apartment.

Once we're all buckled into the car, Theo presses some buttons, turning up the heat. We're in a large SUV this time. He usually picks me up in a Range Rover. I don't know what kind of car this one is, but it's about twice the size of the other one.

"Where are we going anyway?" I ask.

"You'll see," is all he says as he takes my hand in his before resting it on his upper leg.

I do my best not to squirm, not to think about what it would feel like to run my fingers up his muscular thigh. My own thighs squeeze closed, and I whimper. Theo eyes me with a heated look as his thumb runs in little circles around the back of my hand. *Damn it*, everything he does is turning me on. I really need to go and get laid, find a willing participant for just one night. Something tells me they wouldn't be anywhere near as good as how I imagine Theo being. Could he even live up to what I picture? I get lost in my thoughts, and before I know it, we're pulling into the parking lot of a Christmas tree farm.

"Um, Theo, this is a Christmas tree farm," I announce the obvious.

"I know. We're getting you and Lilah a tree, before we stop at a store for decorations, and then we're going to spend the day putting it all together."

I'm speechless. Why would he want to put up a Christmas tree with me and my sister? "Why?" I ask the question my mind can't seem to answer.

"Because you don't have one. Everyone needs a tree in their home, bambolina." He jumps out of the car and I turn my head to my sister.

We haven't had a tree for the last few years, neither of us wanting to put one up without our parents being there. It was something we always did as a family. Lilah has a lost look in her eyes and I know she's thinking the same thing I am. "I can tell him no, Lilah. We don't have to do this."

"No, I think it's time we start making some new family traditions. Mom and Dad wouldn't want us avoiding the holidays," she says, opening her door at the same time Theo opens mine and holds out his hand to me. My arm shakes as I place my palm in his. He looks at it, then up to my eyes, which I can't seem to keep from watering.

"What's wrong?" he asks in a deep, gruff voice while looking around in every direction.

"Nothing. It's just…" I take a breath and glance at Lilah. "We haven't celebrated Christmas since our parents died," I tell him.

"Shit, fuck. Maddie, I'm sorry. I didn't know. We don't have to do this. We can do something else— anything else. Anything you girls want to do."

"No, it's okay. We should start celebrating things again. Let's do this." I don my best fake smile but even I can tell it's weak.

"Are you sure?" Theo stares at me, then Lilah. And damn it, my heart does a little flip as he considers our turbulent emotional states.

"Yep. We're sure," I answer for both of us.

"Can I cut it down?" Lilah asks.

"No," Theo and I say at the same time. He wraps an arm around my shoulders and pulls me into his side as we follow my sister to the entrance. That's when I notice three men, all dressed in those expensive black suits I've become accustomed to seeing. "Lilah, pick out which tree you want, then the guys are going to cut it down and deliver it to the apartment," Theo instructs before he turns to me. "How long can we stay outside?" he whispers, so Lilah doesn't hear his question.

"Fifteen minutes, tops," I'm quick to reply, though I'm not certain of that number. I just assume it's better to play it safe.

"Okay."

We follow Lilah through the farm. It doesn't take long for her to choose a small-looking pine tree, and I'm suddenly thankful for how practical she's being. We can't fit anything much larger in our tiny apartment. When we get to the counter, I pull out my wallet. I don't know how much these trees are, but I'll just pick up longer shifts at the bar or something over the holiday to compensate for the splurge.

Theo frowns at me when he sees I have my debit card in my hands. Snatching it right out of my grasp, he shoves it back into my bag. "Don't ever pull that out again when you're with me," he growls.

"You're not buying me a tree, Theo," I argue.

"I can and I am. In fact, I already have. It's been paid for. Let's go." He grabs my hand and nods for Lilah to walk ahead of us. I haven't missed how he's kept her within his line of sight. I don't know if it's intentional or not, but it's a sweet gesture. That being said, it doesn't make up for his present attitude. I yank my hand out of his and stomp my way to the car. I don't wait for him before I tug the heavy door open and climb in. I also don't miss the laugh he lets out as he walks around to the other side. Once we're on the road again, he says, "Just so we're clear, bambolina, when we get to the department store, I am paying."

I turn in my seat. "We don't need your charity, Theo. I'm more than capable of taking care of things myself. You are not paying for our decorations, and I will find out how much that tree costs and pay you back."

"Maddie, it's not that I don't think you're capable of taking care of yourself and your sister. Clearly, you are. I *want* to do this. Besides, it's not a good look for me, allowing you to pay for shit."

"It's not a good look? Seriously, Theo, I don't care what kind of look it is. It's not a good look for me to have people think I'm your kept mistress."

"You're far from a kept mistress, bambolina." He smirks.

"You're absolutely right. A mistress would at least let you fuck her."

He glares at me and his fingers tighten around the steering wheel.

"You know what? I think we should go for green and purple decorations," Lilah calls out from the back seat. The rest of the ride to the store is silent.

CHAPTER 12

Theo

I've never been more nervous in my life driving into my family's estate. After we spent a few hours in the store, we loaded up the back of the SUV and went to Maddie's. It took us the better part of the day to set up the tree.

Maddie was silently fuming that I yet again paid for the bill for the decorations. And I heard all about how pissed she was when Lilah excused herself to nap for an hour before we left for dinner. I let her get everything out, rant and rave about how she's an independent woman and didn't need a man to look after her. When she was finished, all I said was that it made me happy to do things for her.

Which is the truth. I don't remember a time I've had more fun than decorating the tree with Maddie and Lilah. When I'm with her, I feel like I can be myself. Truly myself. Although, the farther we drive into the estate, the more I feel my mask slipping back over my face. This isn't a place where I can relax; it's where I need to make sure shit is getting done. Where responsibility upon responsibility is thrust on my shoulders. Don't get me wrong, I love my family. I love my role within it. I just sometimes wish I hadn't been born first.

I can see Maddie fidgeting with the hem of her dress. I squeeze her hand reassuringly. "Are you okay?" I ask her.

"What if they don't like me? I mean, I yelled at your dad on the phone, Theo. I made a fool of myself."

"What the fuck is there not to like? Besides, I like you plenty and that's all that matters," I tell her. I couldn't care less if my family approves or not. It'd be easier if they did. We do spend a lot of fucking time together. But I'm not about to let Maddie go anywhere if they don't like her.

"Awww, so sweet. I can't wait until I find a guy just like you, Theo. But younger. Wait, you have younger brothers, right?" Lilah says from the back seat.

"Fuck no, Lilah… She's not serious, is she? She doesn't date, right? Surely she's too young for that?" I ask Maddie, who just laughs at my obvious distress. I don't know why but the idea of Lilah—sweet little Lilah—*dating* makes my blood boil. I barely know the girl but I can't deny the strong protective instinct I have when it comes to her. One that I can't hide.

"Lilah, his brothers are way too old for you. Remember: best behavior, manners, etc." Maddie turns to her sister.

"Just be yourself. You'll be fine, and stay away from my brothers. If they bother you, come and tell me."

"Oh, I'm sure they won't be a bother." Lilah winks as she opens the door. And I groan while opening mine. By the time I walk around to Maddie's side, she's already out of the car.

"Ready?" I hold my hand out to her. She looks at my outstretched palm like she's considering whether or not to take it. Relief washes over me when she chooses the former.

"Wow, this is really where you grew up?" Lilah asks, amazed at the grandeur of the home.

"Yep," I say. "Come on, everyone will be in the dining room." I lead them towards the back of the house, ignoring all the looks from the soldiers and house staff we pass along the way.

The conversations grow louder the closer we get, and I shake my head when I recognize my uncle's voice. Of course, Dad would make this an entire family event. I stop and turn to Maddie. "Whatever my Uncle Neo or Aunt Angelica have to say tonight, ignore them. They're both fucking crazy as fuck."

Her eyes widen and her hand grips mine tighter.

Does it make me an ass that I like how she seeks comfort from me? How she holds onto me tighter when she's unsure of something? I don't care what the fuck that makes me. Walking through the door of the dining room, I see that everyone is already seated at the table. The whole room goes silent as we approach the threshold. Talk about making an entrance.

My mom's the first one on her feet as she rushes over to us. "Theo, finally! I've been waiting for hours," she says. Instead of hugging me like she usually does, she goes straight for Maddie. "You must be Maddie. You're even more beautiful than my son said you were." Then she engulfs her in a hug.

"I never told you how beautiful she is, Mom," I say.

"No, you didn't. But your brother did." She smiles and I send Matteo a glare. "And you must be Lilah." Mom hugs Lilah. "Come, sit down, dinner is almost ready."

What the fuck? Am I chopped liver? Where the fuck is my greeting? I don't say anything as I lead Maddie over to the table while my mother takes Lilah, seating the girl beside her. "Maddie, this is my father—everyone calls him T. And, Pops, this is Maddie," I introduce them.

"H-hello, Mr. Valentino," Maddie says quietly.

"It's just T, sweetheart. It's a pleasure to meet

you," Dad says with a charming smile, his eyes bouncing between the two girls.

I introduce her to my brothers next. "Unfortunately, you already know Matteo. This is Luca and that's Romeo." I point to each and they say hello. "This is my Uncle Neo and my Aunt Angelica." I gesture to the couple to my left.

"It's great to meet you, Maddie and Lilah," Aunt Angelica says. My uncle is just staring at them though. I look to Pops, to see what the fuck is happening. Uncle Neo is never this quiet.

I'm about to walk straight back out the door with Maddie and Lilah in tow, when my dad's voice breaks the awkward silence. "Neo, Theo, I need a word with both of you in my office."

"Now? Can't it wait?" I ask.

"Now." My father stands and walks out of the room, stopping to whisper something in my mother's ear.

"I'm sorry. This won't take long," I tell Maddie, pulling her chair out. I give Matteo a look that says everything I don't: *Keep an eye on her for me.* He nods his head in understanding, and I follow my father and uncle out of the room.

"Ah, T, what the fuck? You're seeing what I'm seeing, right?" my uncle says the moment we cross the threshold, turning the surveillance monitors on and flicking straight to the camera that shows the dining room.

"It's uncanny. It has to be a coincidence. There's no fucking way," my father replies ominously.

"Ah, anyone want to share with me what the fuck you two are talking about?" I run a hand through my hair, frustrated as fuck at the both of them.

"What did you say Maddie's surname was?" my father asks instead of explaining.

"I didn't," I answer him.

"Don't be an ass, Theo. What the fuck is that girl's surname?"

"Why?" I'm not about to give them any more info if they have an issue with her. He doesn't answer. He does, however, open a cabinet door and pull out an old photo album. Flipping through the pages, he finds what he's looking for, removes something, and hands it to me. I look at the photo of a young girl about Lilah's age smiling at the camera. But she's not just Lilah's age; she's the spitting fucking image of the girl. "Who is this?"

"That's Lana. She was our best friend growing up," my father says.

"She ran off and married a Russian. War broke out, and she and her husband went into hiding. We couldn't find them anywhere," Uncle Neo adds. "All this time we thought they were dead."

I recall Maddie telling me her father was Russian, her mother Italian. If she really is the daughter of whom my father thinks she is, then Maddie and Lilah are mafia royalty. On both sides… "Their parents are dead. They died a few years ago, but I never pried into what happened," I admit.

I can see that I just dashed their hopes that their friend was still alive. "What is their last name?" my father asks again.

"Smith," I tell him, only now realizing how the name is such an obvious fake.

"Right. Let's go back out there. Not a word about this to either of them. If they don't know their heritage, there's a reason their parents didn't want them to know."

"Right," I agree. Fuck, have I put Maddie and Lilah in danger by bringing them around me? I don't care what I have to do. I will not let anything happen to them.

"Lilah, I'll meet you upstairs," Maddie says to her sister when I pull up out front of her apartment. Dinner went as well as can be expected—with my brothers there to give me shit and doing their best to embarrass me. Once Lilah is out of the car and safely in the building, Maddie turns to me. "What's wrong?"

"What do you mean? Nothing's wrong," I answer.

"Bullshit, you've been unusually quiet all night."

"I have to go away for Christmas with my family. To Canada," I say.

"You're upset that you're spending Christmas in Canada? What a sad, sad life you must have."

"No, I'm upset that I won't get to see you for a couple of weeks," I admit.

"Oh," she says, biting into her bottom lip. "When do you leave?"

"Tuesday."

"Okay. Well, you know, you can always Facetime me, if you want..."

"You and Lilah could come with me," I suggest instead.

"We can't leave. Lilah has her dialysis treatments."

"I can have a doctor and everything she needs wherever we are."

"I'm sure you can, but this is the first holiday we've actually celebrated since our parents died. I think it would be better if it were just the two of us."

Fuck, I know it makes sense for them to spend it together, without all the added stress of being around complete strangers. However, it doesn't mean I like it. "What happened to your parents?" I ask, now more curious than I ever was before.

"They died in a car crash... A drunk driver hit them," she says.

I don't know why but I'm relieved. A drunk

driver does not sound like a mob hit. That means these two girls probably don't have two extremely resourceful families looking for them. "I'm sorry."

"Theo?"

"Yeah?"

"I'll see you in two weeks. Have fun with your family." She leans over the center of the car and her lips slam down over mine.

I'm stunned for a whole two seconds before I take control, my hand snaking around the back of her neck and holding her to me. I've been waiting weeks for this fucking kiss. I'm not about to let her stop it anytime soon. My tongue slides into her mouth, and a groan rumbles through my chest as I taste her. Fuck, I need her. Picking her up, I pull her over the center console so she's now straddling me. "Fuck, bambolina, you have no idea how much I've wanted to fucking kiss you."

"I think I have an idea." She smiles at me. "I gotta go. Call me if you want." She climbs back over to the passenger's side, and before I can get my mouth to form words, she's gone.

CHAPTER 13

Maddie

It's been a week since Theo left, a week since I've felt his lips on mine. I can't believe I kissed him. I made that move. I gave in to what my body so desperately wanted and fused my lips with his. Not that he seemed to mind at all, judging by the hardness I felt against my core when he so effortlessly lifted me over the center of the car and forced me to straddle his lap.

Jesus, I need to get a grip.

It was just a kiss. That's what I keep telling myself anyway. It means nothing. What could I possibly expect to happen between us? He's a goddamn mob boss, and I'm a waitress with a little sister to care for. Which brings me to why I'm currently standing out front of a seedy-looking strip club. Turns out that little trip to the hospital a few weeks ago cost more than I thought it would.

The bill arrived at my doorstep three days ago. I spent the first day ignoring it, the next crying in the shower and pretending I was fine in front of everyone. And now, here I am. Looking for some form of employment that will hopefully pay more than both of my current jobs put together. I found out about this place from Anna, the other morning barista at Grind the Bean. She said the tips are in the thousands, and all the waitresses have to do is serve drinks in their underwear.

I can do that. It's not like they'll pay me much attention anyway, right? Surely the slimy-ass men who frequent this place will be focused on the girls who are actually on the stage dancing, rather than the girls serving them drinks. *I can do this*, I repeat internally. I need to do this. This is what you do for your family. Whatever it takes.

Pushing my shoulders back, and with my head held high, I walk through the doors. I'm stunned by the opulence. I was expecting... Well, I'm not sure what I was expecting, but it wasn't *this*. There're three stages around the room, cages hang from the ceiling, and plush red velvet booths are scattered around, each with a view to the various stages. The place is empty, but I can imagine it full of patrons, dimmed lighting, and naked women.

I make my way over to the bar, where a young guy is eyeing me with caution. "Hi, I have an interview with Samuel." I'm proud of myself for managing to get that out without any waver in my voice.

"Yeah, I think you should turn around and walk straight back out that door, sweetheart. This ain't the place for you," he says.

"Are you Samuel?" I ask.

"Nope." He pops his P. "Thankfully," he adds under his breath.

"Well, if you could go let him know that I'm here, or point me in the direction of where I might be able to find him, that'd be great."

"Don't say I didn't warn you," he replies before disappearing through a door at the back of the bar. I look down at myself. I'm wearing a pair of faded jeans and a thick black coat, black gloves, and a pink scarf. I know I probably look like crap—my eye bags have bags at this point. However, I don't have time to dwell on my appearance before a big beefy guy with a huge-ass beard steps up next to me.

"You must be Maddie, welcome. Come on through to the back and we'll start your interview," he says, giving me a once-over with his eyes then turning around and walking off. I follow behind him. What choice do I have? I need this job, and as much as my gut is telling me to run out that front door and never come anywhere near this place, I can't. I make my feet take one step after the other. I trail the man, who I'm assuming is Samuel, into a little office. He sits behind a desk and points to a chair. "Have a seat. This won't take long."

"Thank you. I appreciate you taking the time to meet with me, Mister... ah, Samuel?" I question, not sure what to call him.

He laughs. "Yeah, sure," he says. "We have an opening on Friday. You want it, it's yours. Be here at seven, not a second later. The girls are all required to wear black dresses. The more skin you show, the more you'll earn."

"O-okay, I can do that."

"Yep, I'm sure you can. I'll add you to the lineup. You can see yourself out," he dismisses me with a wave of his hand.

The whole way home, I replay that meeting over and over. I wouldn't exactly call it an interview, and frankly, I'm not even sure what the hell I've signed myself up for. When I arrive at my apartment building, I find Gia and Lilah on the sofa watching *Legally Blonde*. My sister is determined she's going to be a lawyer one day and says Elle Woods is the best fictional character of all time.

"Hey, how are you feeling?" I ask Lilah. She had her treatment today.

"Good. Where've you been?"

I'm home later than I usually would be. "Ah, the train was delayed," the lie slips from my mouth near effortlessly and I hate myself for breaking our promise to each other. But I can't tell her about the strip club. Friday is only three days away. I'll go, find out what the job is all about, and then I'll be able to see if I really can do it or not. How much worse can it be than working at the bar? I'll just be serving drinks, in a black dress. Which reminds me, I need to find a black dress by Friday...

"I'm going to shower," I call over my shoulder. Twenty minutes later, I walk back out to the living room. "Where's Lilah?" I ask Gia.

"She went to study in her room," she says, giving me her *I know you're hiding something* look.

"Don't look at me like that." I plop myself down on the sofa next to her and lean my head on her shoulder.

"Well, I wouldn't have to if you told me what it is you're hiding."

"I'm not hiding anything," I deny.

"Yeah, sure you're not. Is it Theo? Is he back yet?"

"Nope, not until next week." Which is good. The last thing I need is him following me to a strip club on Friday.

"Right, so if it's not Theo, then what is it? Wait, did you guys do phone sex?"

I laugh. As much as Theo has tried to persuade

me to do just that, we haven't. I refuse to have phone sex with someone I haven't even had real-life sex with. Not that I'm planning to have real-life sex with Theo... I have to admit it has been kind of nice getting to know him over text messages and short phone calls. "I have a new job," I blurt, sighing once I've put it out into the world.

"Doing what?" Gia asks.

"Waitressing." Not a lie... I will be waitressing.

"Okay, where at?"

This is when I pause. I know I should tell her. I should tell someone where I'll be, just in case something happens and she needs to find me. "Ah, it's a little club in the city."

"What's the name of this *little club* and why are you being so evasive about it?"

"I'm not being evasive. It's called Club S. It's a strip club but I'm not stripping—I swear—just waitressing."

"No, you can't be serious. Why the hell would you want to do that?"

"It's not that I want to. It's more of a necessity. I have a pile of bills on the counter with *overdue* and *payment needed* stamps on them. I can't afford not to."

"I don't think this is a good idea, Maddie. Do you know the kind of people who frequent those types of clubs?"

"Probably a bunch of harmless old men, G. It'll be

fine. But I do need to borrow a little black dress for Friday night."

"Why do I feel like this is how every documentary starts where the girl ends up missing? *She just wanted to earn some extra money, and the next thing we knew, she was gone?*" She sighs.

"Well, if I go missing, look after Lilah for me, will you." I smirk.

"You know I will," she says. "So, what does Mr. Tall-Dark-and-Solid think about this new job of yours? Can't imagine that possessive caveman would approve."

"It doesn't matter what he thinks. I'm the only boss of me, G. Also, he doesn't have to know."

"Yeah, okay." She rolls her eyes.

Climbing into bed after my shift at the bar, I sigh in relief. My whole body is tired, sore, and overworked. I have four hours before I have to be up in the morning. Just as I plug my phone into the charger, it lights up with the name *Theo* on the screen. Smiling, I unplug it and answer the video call. "Hey there? How's the snow?" I ask.

"Cold. It'd be a lot better if you were here to

warm me up, bambolina." His smooth, deep voice sends sparks right to my core.

"I'm sure you can afford heating. What'd you do today?"

"Not much. What'd you get up to?"

"Worked, hung out with Gia and Lilah, and then worked again," I say.

"What are your plans for Christmas Day?" he asks.

Christmas is Saturday. The day after my first shift at Club S. "Mmm, I'm working Christmas Eve so probably not a lot. Just hang out with Lilah I guess. You?"

"You're working Christmas Eve? Where?"

"The bar," I lie. Although, judging by the look he's giving me, he's not buying it. The bar's closed for Christmas weekend, but there's no way he'd know that. "Shit, Theo, my phone's going dead. I gotta go. Talk later." I hang up before he can question me any further, then quickly switch my phone off so he can't call me back.

CHAPTER 14
Theo

I keep thinking about the phone call with Maddie last night, and how she's not answering my calls or messages today. I know she's at work. I've had a few guys go into the coffee shop to check on her. I also know she's lying about working at the bar on Christmas Eve. I paid the owner a large sum of fucking money to close down over the holiday weekend. Maddie needs a break. She works way too fucking much. If I thought she'd accept it, I'd give her an account so she wouldn't have to struggle to support herself. Move her and Lilah straight into my penthouse. Give them everything they could ever want.

She's not there yet and I don't want to push her. I'm also waiting to find out what the fuck my father and uncle plan to do about the girls' lineage. Will bringing them farther into my world put a bigger target on their backs? Will either side of their families recognize them? Would they want to know they're legacy—the crime families each of their parents came from?

I have no fucking idea. What I do know is that I'm not about to let Maddie go… I can't. And I am also going to find out where the fuck she plans on working on Christmas Eve.

I pull out my phone to call her friend Gia to see what she'll tell me. Probably nothing. She's fucking loyal to a fault. It's worth a shot though. Before I can connect the call, though, Matteo barges into my room and falls dramatically onto my bed.

"What the fuck are you doing in here?"

"I think I fucked up. Like really, really fucked up," he says, draping an arm over his eyes.

"What'd you do?" I ask. Knowing him, it could be fucking any number of things. When he doesn't answer, I pour myself a drink from the wet bar. Something tells me I'm going to need it. "Matteo, I can't fix your fucking messes if you don't tell me what the fuck you did?"

"Yeah, not even you can fix this one, bro," he groans.

"Well, if you're not going to tell me and you don't want my help, then get the fuck out of my room. I have shit to do."

"I got married," he blurts out, sitting upright and looking at me with wide eyes.

I don't think I've heard him correctly. Because there is no fucking way… "Say that again, because I swear I just heard you say you got fucking married."

"That's what I said."

"What the fuck, Matteo? When? To whom?"

He falls back down onto the bed. "Two weeks ago in Vegas… to Savvy," he groans.

This makes me laugh. "Did you drug her? How the fuck did you end up married to Savannah?"

"I didn't fucking drug her. We were drunk. I don't remember all the details."

"Okay, so what? You've been in love with her forever. You guys are best friends. I'm sure you can make it work." I have no words, no idea what the fuck I'm supposed to say to that.

"She wants a divorce, or an annulment or some shit."

"So give her one." I shrug.

"I can't."

"You can't or you won't. They are two completely different things, Matteo."

"I won't. What if this is the only chance I'll ever get at keeping her?"

"Jesus Christ, she's not a fucking doll you get to lock away in a tower somewhere and pull out when you feel like it."

"I know that," he growls. "I just… I want to keep her," he says again.

"What about what she wants?" I know Savannah

has feelings for my dumbass brother. She always has. She's just too scared to cross that line, ruin their friendship, and lose him.

"She wants me, obviously. What's not to want? She just won't admit it. But fuck, I've never been with anyone like her. I might not remember much of that night, but I do remember the important part and it was fucking epic."

"I don't want to know." I cringe at the image.

"What am I going to do?"

"No idea. Do Mom and Dad know?" I ask him.

"Do I look stupid?"

"You really want me to answer that?"

"Nope. And, no, they don't know."

"Maybe start by breaking the news to them—you know, that they now have a daughter-in-law."

"Argh, fuck my life," Matteo groans.

For once, I would not want to be in my brother's shoes. When our parents find out he went and married Savannah in Vegas, they are going to lose it. I think my mom's been planning their wedding since they were in kindergarten together. And my dad? Yeah, he's going to be pissed Matteo did something so careless. He loves Savannah like she's his own daughter. If she really wanted out of this marriage, all she'd have to do was talk to Pops and he'd make it happen. No questions asked. The fact she hasn't done that shows she doesn't actually want out. What she wants is for Matteo to grow the fuck up and prove to her that he's ready for that level of commitment. That it wasn't just an impulsive decision.

I hope for both of their sakes that he fucking is, and that it wasn't.

The day gets away from me, between talking Matteo off a cliff and then being the peacemaker when he came clean and faced our parents at the fucking dinner table. Let's just say it was fucking chaos.

I'm currently sitting out on the balcony. It's freezing fucking cold, and the whiskey I'm drinking does nothing to alleviate the chill. But at least from here I can see the stars. Staring up at the sky, I try to call Maddie again. And, again, the call goes straight to voicemail. My phone immediately pops up with a text.

MADDIE:

Sorry. I'm exhausted. Talk tomorrow. xx

ME:

Why the fuck are you avoiding me, bambolina?

My question gets read but she doesn't respond.

"Fuck!" I throw my glass out into the yard. I watch as it lands on the snow. The piece of shit doesn't even fucking shatter.

"What did that whiskey do to you?" Alex sits down next to me. I glare at him but don't bother answering.

"Girl troubles?" he asks with a raised brow.

"She's avoiding me," I admit.

"Well, with your charming personality, I don't see why any woman in their right mind would want to avoid you, Theo." The fucker laughs.

"Is there a reason you're coming out here interrupting my peace?"

"Didn't look too peaceful to me."

Again I ignore him and look up into the stars. "Ever get sick of this life?"

"Every fucking day," he groans. "But then, this is who we are. Do you think we'd be able to settle for a nine-to-five?"

"Nope. But what if this job is what costs me my girl?" I finally ask the question out loud. What if who I am is too much for Maddie to handle?

"Then she's not the right girl for you to begin with," Alex says. "Look, you're not a bad guy, Theo, and if she can't see that, then that's her loss."

"Yeah, maybe," I say. With everything that's happened today, I never got the chance to call Gia or dig into what Maddie's been up to. And the guys I have following her at a distance have all come up empty. Said they lost her for about an hour the other day, but don't know where she went. I didn't even know she knew she was being followed—obviously if she went out of her way to give the guys the slip, she knew they were there. And she's doing something she doesn't want me to know about.

The thing is this is fucking New York City, and I fucking own it. One way or another, I'll find out what she has her hands in. I just hope it's not too fucking late when I do.

"I gotta make a call. Good chat." I stand and walk back inside. I hear Alex's laughter follow me. Shutting myself in my room, I find Gia's number and connect the call. It almost rings out when she finally picks up.

"Hello," her sleepy voice answers.

"Gia, it's Theo. What the fuck is Maddie doing on Friday night?" I get straight to the point.

"Theo, it's two in the morning. Why are you calling me?"

"I need to know what Maddie is doing Friday night," I tell her.

"So call her and ask."

"She's avoiding me. I know she tells you everything. What is she doing?"

"OMG, look, it's not my place to say. She's just got a new job waitressing—that's all. If she's avoiding your calls, then maybe you should get the hint that she doesn't want to speak to you?"

Ignoring her rant, I press on, "Where is this wait-ressing job?"

"I don't know. I gotta go." She hangs up.

Fuck! I don't know what it is, but something is not sitting right. I know my parents are going to give me fucking grief for leaving before Christmas, but I need to get back to New York. Picking up my suit-case, I fill it with everything I need while calling the pilot, instructing him to have the plane ready to take me back to the city in half an hour.

I don't step foot on New York soil until the next day—the fucking plane was grounded due to weather. By the time we could actually fly, it was midday on Friday. To say I was pissed was an under-statement. As soon as I slip into the back seat of the waiting SUV, I call Anthony. He's been tailing Maddie all day.

"Where is she?" I ask him.

"Ah, boss, she... um... she..." he stumbles over his words and my stomach drops.

"Anthony, where the fuck is she?" I hiss into the phone, my tone firm.

"She just walked into Club S," he says.

"And you fucking let her?" I yell. *Fucking Club S.*

You've got to be shitting me. There is no fucking way I'm letting this happen. Club S is a strip club, but it's also a front for an auction house—an *establishment* where sick fucks bid for women. Innocent women, like fucking Maddie.

Waitressing, my ass. Does she know what she's walking into? Is she really going to let herself be auctioned off to the highest fucking bidder?

"Boss?" Anthony calls down the line.

"I'm on my way. Do not let her out of your fucking sight," I shout. Twenty minutes later, the driver pulls up to the building in question. I see four of my men standing out front, waiting for me. Acknowledging them with a nod, I storm inside.

Someone's head is about to fucking roll.

CHAPTER 15
Maddie

My nerves are rattled as hell as I walk into the dark club. Approaching the bar, I lean over and ask where I can find Samuel. There're a few men behind the bar. There are several women in black dresses walking around the club with drink trays in the air, while multiple others are dancing on the stages. And when I look up, the cages are all occupied by couples. The waitresses, though, don't look like they're having any trouble with the patrons. I don't think this is going to be anywhere near as bad as I was thinking.

The guy behind the bar tells me to head to the back, so I make my way to the same office from the other day. Knocking on the door, I hear a deep voice yell out, "It's open." I pull down on the handle and push forward, then stand on the threshold and wait for the big burly man to look up at me. "You made it

—on time too." He nods to a girl who's sitting on the sofa that's off to the side of the room. "Cindy will show you to the dressing room. Once you've put your stuff away, go and see Carl at the bar. He'll give you your section."

"Thank you."

An hour later, my feet are burning in the stilettos I'm wearing. But there has not been a single incident. None of the men have tried to grope me. Not one of them has made a crude comment. Nothing but drink orders. Maybe I built this up in my head, making it into something that it's clearly not. Just as I'm considering my possible misjudgment, the overhead lights spring to life, the girls that were dancing on the platforms disappear behind the curtains, and Samuel walks out onto the center stage with a microphone in hand.

Confused, I look around. Everyone has stopped talking. The waitresses stand frozen to their spots. *What the hell is going on?*

"It's that time, gentlemen. We have some fine stock for you tonight. Bidding starts at 20K. You know the rules."

Bidding? What is he talking about? A spotlight

circles the room, round and round, going from one waitress to the next. Then it stops on me.

"It's only fair to start tonight's auction with fresh meat. Meet Maddie, first time here. Who's going to get us started at 20K?" Samuel's voice booms through the crowded space and paddles start flying up from the tables.

I scan my surroundings but my feet won't move. It takes a while for my brain to catch up with me, to figure out just what's happening in the moment. What the fuck did I get myself into? Though the better question is how the fuck am I going to get myself out of it?

The static of the microphone breaks through my panic. "We have one hundred and fifty. Do I hear one-fifty-five?"

Who the hell is prepared to pay one hundred and fifty thousand dollars for me? That's insane. *Laughable.* Whoever it is they're wasting their money, because I'm not sticking around any longer. Finally my feet start to move. I need to get out of here. I make it five steps before two men stop me in my tracks, each grabbing hold of one of my arms.

I yank my limbs back and scream. "No, let me go. This is a mistake. Stop. Let me go." I may as well be begging to two sets of deaf ears. They don't budge. Tears are now falling down my cheeks. Great, just what I need. I have to think. To figure a way out of here. I stomp my heel down on one of the guys' feet. He curses but his grip doesn't waver. Fuck.

"Three-hundred thousand," a deep voice calls out over the crowd. A voice I know all too well. Looking up, I stare straight into the eyes of Mr. Tall-Dark-and-*Furious*. His face is as hard as stone, his eyes darker than I've ever seen them. "You have exactly three seconds to remove your hands from her before I cut your fingers off and shove them up your fucking ass," he grits out through clenched teeth and a firmly set jaw, the hissed threat directed at the two men at my side. "Too late," he adds *exactly three seconds* later. And before I know what's happening, I hear the unmistakable sound of two gunshots. One after the other.

I scream, stumbling to the floor as I take cover. The two men are gone, and my arms are free. What the hell is going on? Straightening, I find Theo staring right at me. He's holding a pistol out, but not directed at me. No, it's aimed at something—someone—behind me. I go to turn around, but his other hand reaches out and grabs my arm, pulling my chest against his.

"If any of you fuckers even thinks about looking in this woman's direction again, I won't just end you. I'll end your whole goddamn fucking family tree." He turns around to face the stage with his barrel still raised, and I shriek when his arm recoils and another gunshot rings out in my ears. My eyes are closed tight, my face buried in Theo's chest. I can feel the fast beat of his heart under my hands, which are currently clinging to his shirt like my life depends on it.

And right now, it kind of seems like it does.

"Let this be your only motherfucking warning," he yells as he pulls me back from his embrace to grab hold of my hand, and I'm dragged behind him as he exits the club.

I'm in shock. I know that. By the time he stops at a waiting car on the street, my whole body is shaking uncontrollably.

"Give me the keys. Get a clean-up crew in here," Theo says to someone, but I don't look up. I can't. My eyes are stuck to the ground. The car door opens and Theo picks me up, placing me on the seat before he leans in and buckles the seat belt around me. He slams his door when he gets into the driver's side, the jarring noise making me jump, and within seconds, he pulls out into the city traffic. Then he's cursing in Italian as he slams his hand on the steering wheel over and over again.

I've never really been afraid of him. Sure, I've been wary because I know who he is. But wary is different from scared, and right now, I'm fucking terrified. I watch as he inhales deeply, then it's like a mask slips over his whole face. It's almost as if he's not here. Not the man I've been getting to know.

"Theo?" I question. I don't know what exactly I

want to say. What can I say? I should thank him. He got me out of that situation. But he shot people. Three people. Right in front of me. Is my life really worth more than theirs? I'm not sure.

"Don't," he grits out. "Just don't speak right now. Jesus-fucking-Christ, Maddie, what the fuck were you thinking?" he yells.

I don't know whether I should answer him or not. He just told me not to speak, then asked me a goddamn question. So, instead, I turn my head and look out the window.

A few minutes later, he huffs, "Why didn't you ask me for help? If you were so desperate for cash that you were prepared to fucking auction yourself off, why didn't you ask me?" He sounds hurt.

"I didn't know. I thought it was just a waitressing job. I wouldn't do that. I wouldn't have been there if I knew."

He doesn't respond as he continues to drive erratically through the traffic. It takes twenty minutes to get to my apartment building instead of the usual forty. I'm a mess. I don't know what to think. What to do. Theo cuts the engine, then turns to me. "This is what's going to happen. You're going to go inside, pack a bag for you and Lilah, and you're going to do it quickly."

"What? Why am I packing a bag?"

"You're both going to be staying at my place. Come on, let's go."

"I can't. We can't. No."

"You don't have a fucking choice, Maddie. I'm not giving you a fucking choice here. I'm done giving you fucking choices. You have no idea the mess you've created tonight."

"The mess *I've* created? Nobody told you to come in guns blazing, Theo. That's on you, not me."

"Maddie, for fuck's sake, just do what I tell you to do. We can argue about this later. Right now, we need to get you and Lilah the fuck out of here."

"Why?"

He doesn't answer, just shakes his head and pinches the bridge of his nose as he gets out of the car and walks around to my side. Opening the passenger door, he waits for me to exit.

"What am I supposed to tell Lilah?"

"Not my problem right now, Maddie. Just tell her we're spending the holiday weekend together or something." The tone of his voice, the way his body is so tense, and how he's looking around everywhere —up and down the street—tells me there is no arguing with him right now. Maybe we are in danger here? That thought alone has me complying with his demands.

Walking into the apartment, I tiptoe into my room, shove as much as I can into a bag, and then do the same for Lilah. She's a heavy sleeper. I look down at her resting peacefully. How do I explain this to her? Shaking her gently, I whisper, "Lilah, wake up. We have to go somewhere."

She rubs at her eyes. "Maddie, what's wrong?" she asks, sitting upright.

"Nothing, but Theo came to pick us up. He wants to take us to his place for the weekend." Another lie.

"Why? Can't he wait until a decent hour?" she whines.

"I'm sorry, Lilah. I'm so sorry," I whisper. I can't tell her what kind of trouble I've gotten myself into, but I can apologize for dragging her down with me.

"It's okay, Maddie. I'm up." She stands and stretches.

"Here, put this on." I hand her a hoodie and then a thick coat. She guides her feet into her slippers. "Come on." I tug her out of the room.

Theo is waiting by the door. He turns around when he sees us, and a bit of his hardness vanishes when he looks at Lilah. However, when his eyes return to mine, all I see reflected back is anger. "Ready?" he asks.

I nod my head in answer and take hold of my sister's hand. She doesn't question anything but she does give my palm a reassuring squeeze. Once we're outside the apartment building, I freeze in front of Lilah when I see three blacked-out SUVs blocking the street.

Theo continues walking to the car, opening both of the passenger doors. It's not until then that he notices I've stopped moving. "Maddie, come on." His voice is calmer, softer than the harsh tone he projected before. Though I assume the change is more for Lilah's benefit than mine.

No one speaks as we drive back into the city, and the tension is almost too much to bear. The events of the night run on replay in my mind. But the one thing that sticks out the most, the thing that's bothering me more than any of the carnage I've witnessed, is the fact that Theo hasn't reached across the console to hold my hand. He always holds my hand in the car.

CHAPTER 16
Theo

I'm doing my best to maintain control of my anger, but it's fucking hard. So fucking hard. When I saw Maddie in the club... saw those two fuckers with their hands on her... heard bid after bid from the fucking men who wanted to win her...

I fucking lost it.

There is no other explanation for why I'd go in and shoot three members of the Gambino family. I'm not stupid. I know what I've done is going to have major backlash. And I know my father would have heard what went down by now. Why he hasn't called yet is anyone's guess.

I pull into my private underground parking lot. The three cars I had tailing us pull in behind me. I have twenty men living in this building. My security team is top notch; there's no way anyone will get in here. I know the repercussions from tonight fall on me. But now that I've made it very public knowledge that Maddie is mine, I have no doubt my enemies will be looking to get to her. What better way to make the unbreakable Theo Valentino crack, than to destroy the thing he holds dearest.

I let all my fucking cards show tonight. This is why I never wanted to fall in love.

Fuck! The tension that filled the car follows us into the elevator as I guide Maddie and Lilah inside. I press my thumb to the panel on the wall, and the elevator starts its climb to the top, moments before the doors open right into my foyer.

"Come on, I'll show you the guest room, Lilah." The girls silently trail behind me. I open the door to the largest guest room, pointing to the adjoining door. "There's a bathroom through there. If you need anything, we'll be straight down the hall."

I don't miss the way Maddie cringes at that. "Okay. Well, I'd love to stay and chat, but it's like the middle of the night." She nods to her sister.

"Do you need anything?" I ask her. Lilah shakes her head. "Okay." I take hold of Maddie's hand and lead her to my room. I've wanted to have her in my bed since the first moment I saw her. However, I never expected to have her here like this. Forced. By my hand and my actions. I could set her up in one of the other guest rooms, but fuck that. She belongs in my fucking bed.

Dropping her hand, I walk into my closet and

pull out a t-shirt. Then I walk back out, take her hand again, and lead her into the bathroom before I turn on the shower, making sure it's warm.

"You can wear this." I pass her the shirt. "There're towels on the shelf behind you." She's covered in blood splatter. I don't think she's even noticed yet. When she doesn't move or say anything, I ask, "Need me to wash you, bambolina?"

"N-n-no." She shakes her head so fast I'm surprised it's not falling off her shoulders.

"Okay, if you need anything, yell out." I push past the door and leave her in the bathroom. My bathroom. I head to the main bathroom and have what must be the world's quickest shower. By the time Maddie emerges from the en suite, I'm already sitting on the bed, my back propped against the headboard. I glance up. She's standing in the middle of the room, looking around while her fingers twist the hem of the shirt she's wearing.

I probably should have let her change into something she packed. I didn't realize how much it would turn me fucking on seeing her in my clothes. "W-where am I sleeping?" she finally asks.

I pull the blankets back on the other side of my bed. "Right here." I can't help the way my lips tip up when her eyes widen.

"I can't sleep in your bed."

"Why the fuck not?"

"Because, right now, it doesn't seem like you even

like me. I can just go and sleep with Lilah." She turns around, and I'm up and holding the bedroom door closed by the time she reaches for the handle.

I push her body up against the wood. My chest pressing into her back. I lean in. "You're right. I don't fucking like you," I growl. Her breath hitches but she doesn't say anything. "I'm fucking infatuated with you. Obsessed with you. You are the first thing I think about in the morning, the last thing on my mind at night. You're always there, in my fucking head. I don't like you, Maddie. I'm in fucking love with you." Spinning her around so she's facing me, I wipe her tear-stained cheeks. "Don't cry, bambolina. I fucking hate seeing you cry."

"I'm sorry. I've made a huge mess of things," she whispers.

"I'll fix it. You just have to trust me. Can you do that?"

She bites into her bottom lip as she nods her head. *Thank fuck.*

I take a step back. I want nothing more than to lean in and kiss her, pick her legs up and grind my cock against her pussy. Fuck. I need to regain some semblance of self-control.

"You're still angry."

"I'm fucking fuming, bambolina, but not at you."

"Are you sure?" she asks.

For fuck's sake. Picking her up, I slam her back against the door and my lips meet hers in a frenzied embrace. My tongue enters her mouth. Fucking heaven. I grind into her mound. "Does this feel like I'm angry at you, Maddie?"

"Well, people can be angry and horny, Theo. It doesn't have to be one or the other." She arches her back, grinding herself on my cock harder.

Fuck me. I can feel her wetness through my briefs. "Do you want me to angry fuck the shit out of you, Maddie? Take all my frustrations out on your pussy. Because I can guarantee if that's what you want, you won't be able to walk tomorrow without a limp." I bite down on her earlobe.

"Oh god," she moans as she continues to grind down on me.

"Fuck it!" I growl, walking over to the bed, and throw her down on it. "I've wanted to see you on this bed since the first day I met you. Now I finally have you here, and I'm not sure where I want to start." My eyes travel up and down her body. The shirt she's wearing is bunched up high on her thighs.

Taking in every inch of perfection sprawled out in front of me, I lick my lips. I know exactly where I'm going to start. I kneel on the bed and spread her legs open, her bare wet pussy now fully on display for me. Begging to be tasted. I lean down, slowly dragging my tongue up from the bottom to the top of her slit. My eyes roll back in my head. I knew she'd be different. I knew she'd be addictive, but fuck…

"I've never tasted a cunt more delicious than this.

Get comfortable, bambolina. I'm going to be down here for a while." *After all, you can't fucking rush such delicacies.*

"Oh god." Her hips jump up off the bed as I swirl my tongue around her hardened nub.

"Theo," I tell her, nibbling as I go.

"Huh?" Her head pops up, her brows drawn in confusion.

"Theo—the name I want to hear you calling out is *Theo*. Do not let any other man's name come out of that pretty mouth of yours or I'll have to gag it."

"Fuck." She lets her head fall back onto the bed and I return to my meal.

Inserting a finger into her pussy, I curl it up, rubbing along that sweet spot while sucking on her clit. Within seconds, she's coming all over me and yelling out my fucking name. Sitting upright, I rub my fingers around my mouth before sucking the juices clean from each. "This is too fucking good to let go to waste," I tell her. After retrieving a condom from the bedside table, I roll it on and line my cock up with her entrance. "Are you ready for this, bambolina?" I ask. She tries to move her hips in an attempt to impale herself. "Before I let you have my cock, I need to hear you say it."

"Say what?"

I can feel her thighs quivering. She wants this. She wants it bad. "That you're mine." I smirk down at her.

"Theo, seriously, fuck me already," she argues.

"If you can't say it, then no. I think I'll wait. You're clearly not ready." As much as it kills me, I start to pull away from her.

She brings her legs up around my waist, locking me in place. "Okay, I'm yours. Now can you hurry up and fuck me already."

"Well, since you asked so nicely," I say as I slam into her right to the hilt. "Fucking hell. Jesus, Maddie," I curse. I pull out and slam right back in. Her legs tighten around my waist as she uses the leverage to lift her hips, rolling them around.

"Shit, Theo," she moans as her body tenses. I don't stop. Grabbing her legs, I remove them from my waist, holding them down so her knees are up near her shoulders as I fuck her right through her orgasm and into her next.

"Your cunt is squeezing my cock so fucking good, bambolina. So fucking tight. That's right... coat me with your cum." I can feel I'm about to come. The tingle runs up my spine and my balls tighten. "Fuck. Yes," I curse as I explode, filling the condom while wishing I had forgone it and coated her pussy walls with my cum instead. I fall on top of her, bearing my weight on my elbows. Once I've caught my breath, I finally roll off her. "Get used to this bed, Maddie, because I'm never fucking letting you leave it," I promise her.

My cock twitches. I want her again already.

Pushing to my feet, I walk into the bathroom and dispose of the condom. I'm disappointed it didn't fucking break. I quickly shake my head. I have no idea where the thought of knocking her up with my kid has come from all of a sudden, but right now it seems like a fucking genius thing to do.

I turn the shower on, then walk back into the bedroom. I hold my hand out to Maddie. "Come on, let's shower."

"Together?" she asks, while covering her body with the shirt I never took off her.

"After what we just did, are you really going to be shy with me now? I just had your cunt on my face, bambolina."

"Well, when you put it so eloquently..." She smirks. I can see she's still unsure. Her hands shake a little as I lead her into the bathroom that's now filled with steam.

"There isn't an inch of you that's not fucking beautiful, Maddie. You have no reason to be shy." I slowly lift the shirt over her head, revealing the most delicate creamy skin and breasts, which are perky with hardened nipples that make my mouth water. My hands cup them, feeling their weight in my palms. "I am going to fucking worship these. It's a tragedy I didn't take my time with them before. That's a mistake I won't be repeating." I lean down and take one nipple in my mouth, my fingers pinching and twisting the other.

"Mhmm, Theo. God," Maddie moans, and I bite down hard. "Ow, fuck."

"Don't call out another man's name, ever, Maddie."

"I didn't," she argues.

"God?" I tilt my head, waiting for her to argue with me. I happen to like our verbal sparring matches, far more than I'll ever admit. Especially to her.

"God isn't a man; he's a deity."

"Still a *he*. Still not me," I growl, pulling her into the shower. I let the warm water wash over us.

CHAPTER 17

Maddie

S unlight streams straight onto my face. I pull the covers up over my head. I'm not ready to face the world yet. Not even close. I burrow myself farther into the softness of the pillow, the sheets feeling so smooth on my skin. That's when my eyes flick open and I remember where I am.

Theo's bed. I slept in Theo's bed. I slept with Theo. I remember the feeling of his arms being wrapped around me. He held me so tight. I've never felt as safe as I did in his arms. *Is it a delusion though? Am I really safe here?* Even as I ask myself this question, I know the answer. As safe as I've ever been. Theo is prepared to go above and beyond to ensure my safety. That was obvious last night.

All these weeks I've been holding back. Afraid that if I really let myself feel what I so clearly feel for him, that it'd be wrong. That he was wrong. What kind of person does that make me? That when I really think about it—what he did last night—I don't care. At the time, I questioned him… But, after just one night in his arms, I'm perfectly content with his actions…

Maybe it was the mind-blowing orgasms he gave me. Yes, *multiple* mind-blowing orgasms. I wouldn't be surprised if I blew a gasket or something, and now I'm blinded by the pure pleasure that man can give me. Pleasure like I've never felt before.

Reaching over to the other side of the bed, I find it cold. He's been up for a while. Why didn't he wake me? What time is it? Sitting upright, I find my phone plugged into a charger on the bedside table. I didn't plug it in. Theo must have done it. The smile that is now plastered on my face at the thoughtfulness of the gesture makes me roll my eyes.

It's just a charger, Maddie, not a big deal.

I stand and find a robe laid across the end of the bed. It's white and fluffy; the softness of the material engulfs me as I wrap it around my body. I follow the sounds of voices down the hall, stopping at Lilah's guest room to find the bed empty. Taking a few more steps, I can hear Lilah and Theo talking so I head in their direction. I find them both in the kitchen. Lilah is wearing an apron while mixing what appears to be pancake batter. Although it looks like there's more batter all over the counter and her hands than there is in the bowl.

"Maddie, Theo is teaching me how to make pancakes." She beams at me.

"Well, I hope he's ready for follow-up lessons." I laugh, to which she just sticks her tongue out at me.

Theo is standing by the stove cooking bacon while wearing just a pair of pajama pants that hang low on his hips. I know I saw him in all his naked glory last night. But, god, this man is fine with a capital F. Broad shoulders, solid pecs, and a six-pack with that delicious V that has my eyes following to where it's guiding my line of sight.

Theo clears his throat as he makes his way over to me. He bends and pecks my lips. My whole body leans towards him as he pulls away. "Morning, Maddie, how'd you sleep?" he asks, running a hand through the strands of my hair.

"Ah, good. You?" I ask.

"Never better. Hope you're hungry." I can't help where my eyes land when he asks that. With a finger, he lifts my head so I'm looking at his face again, then he whispers, "For food, bambolina. Not me, although I'm not opposed to taking you back to bed and fucking you all day."

A moan escapes my mouth. Lilah's laugh breaks through my desire-fizzled brain. "Really? You'd think you two would be worn out after last night's show. I think half of New York heard you guys." She grins in my direction.

My whole face heats with embarrassment and I

hide it in Theo's chest as he wraps his arms around me. "Sorry, not sorry," Theo replies to Lilah. "Come sit down. I'll get you a coffee." He leads me over to the counter and sits me on a stool.

My eyes trail down his back—shit, right to his solid ass. I groan. God, I'm losing it. He has *effectively* fried my brain.

"Merry Christmas," Theo says, handing me a holiday-themed coffee mug full to the brim.

"Oh, it's Christmas. Shit, Lilah, I left your gift at the apartment. I'm so sorry."

"It's fine. I don't need gifts. I have you. That's enough for me," she says with a nod, though I still feel like crap about not having something for her to open.

"I'll have someone swing by and pick up whatever else you need, bambolina."

I don't miss the little snicker Lilah releases at the pet name. "Baby doll, huh. It's kind of fitting actually," she says.

"I thought so," Theo agrees.

The rest of breakfast is filled with easy conversation and delicious food. I'm so stuffed I can barely move.

"We're expected at my grandmother's for lunch," Theo says casually, like he just told me he likes his whiskey on ice.

"What?" I shriek.

"My grandmother wants us to go there for lunch."

"I can't possibly eat another thing today. But Lilah and I can go home. You go visit your nonna."

Theo glares at me, his jaw tense. Running his hand through his hair, he exhales harshly, opens his mouth, then closes it again before he stands and silently walks away. I watch him disappear down the hall. He stops when he's at the halfway point, then spins on his heels and charges towards me, making it to his starting point within seconds. He leans over, one hand landing on the back of my chair, the other on the dining table.

"I don't know how much clearer to make this, Maddie. You're not ever going back to that fucking apartment. Get used to calling this place home, bambolina." His voice is barely audible. He then straightens and marches back down the hall. "We're leaving in half an hour," he calls out right before a door slams.

"Well, that was hot," Lilah says, fanning her face dramatically. "What'd he whisper to you?"

I look at her. She seems different. Lighter somehow. "Are you okay? You'd tell me if you wanted to go home, right?"

"Maddie, stop. Look at this place. Why would I want to leave? Also, it makes me feel better knowing you have someone. For when I'm not around anymore. At least you won't be alone."

My heart hurts, hearing her say *that*, realizing she even thinks like *that*. I refuse to entertain the idea that she's not going to make it. "I'm not letting you go anywhere, Lilah. Get dressed. It seems we're meeting more of Theo's family."

With my stomach churning from nerves, I turn the handle to Theo's bedroom, half expecting it to be locked, but it opens. I enter and shut the door at the same time Theo walks out of the bathroom with a towel wrapped low on his hips. Water droplets drip from his hair down his torso.

Angry, you're angry with him, Maddie. I mentally remind myself why I'm here. In this room. And it's not to drool and swoon over him. No matter how much a work of art his body is, I won't let anyone think it's okay to talk to me the way he did. "You have anger problems. You should probably see a therapist or something about that," I tell him.

He laughs—a rich, deep sound that vibrates through me. Shit, not good. "Bambolina, the only person who ever ruffles my feathers is you. I don't have anger problems. I have a problem controlling my emotions around you."

"Why?"

"Why? Because I'm trying to do everything I can to keep you and Lilah safe. And you're dead set on fighting me at every fucking turn."

I follow him into his closet, only to let my eyes wander for a second when he drops his towel. The smirk on his overly gorgeous face tells me he knows exactly what he's doing. "I'm not a dog, Theo. I'm not one of your goons, or soldiers, or minions—whatever it is you call those guys. I'm not someone you can just order around and expect me to say: *yes, sir*. Besides, you don't actually want that. Because if you did, you could get it from any bimbo in this city."

"What I want is you. Kept in one fucking piece, Maddie. Is that really so much to ask?"

"You can't stop whatever fate is intended to come my way. You can't predict the future. All we can do is live for today."

"Well, *today*, I choose to fucking keep you safe. There is a lot of shit going on that I can't tell you about. I need you to trust me."

"We can't stay cooped up in this penthouse forever. Lilah and I can't just move in here with you, Theo."

"Why the fuck not?" he asks, shoving a shirt over his head. He's already put on a pair of dark-navy dress pants.

Why not? I'm trying to rack my brain for a suitable reason as to why we can't do just that. "Lilah has treatments in Brooklyn three times a week. I'm not making her travel that far."

"I've arranged for Doc to start giving her dialysis here. He'll be onsite first thing in the morning, to set up everything in the theater room."

"The theater room?"

"I thought she'd be more comfortable in there. She can binge watch TV or whatever. Doc said the process takes a few hours."

He really has put a lot of thought into this plan of his. Why is my heart doing that little flip thing again? "That has to be costing you a fortune, Theo. We can't ask that of you."

"You didn't ask. And Doc is on retainer, so don't worry about it."

I've been wanting to ask about how the testing of his men has been going. I haven't brought it up because, well, what if it was all talk? What if there is no match?

"We are going to find her a match, bambolina. She will get better and live a full life," he says, as if reading my thoughts.

"You can't know that."

"Haven't you figured it out yet, Maddie?"

"Figured what out?"

"I'm Theo Valentino. I always get what I fucking want." He smirks.

CHAPTER 18
Theo

"Y ou look fucking gorgeous. Stop fidgeting," I lean in and tell Maddie as she locks my hand in a tight grip. She's so hard to fucking read sometimes. One minute she's telling me I don't own her and can't boss her around, and the next she's clinging to me like I'm her fucking lifeline.

"What if your grandmother doesn't like me?" she asks.

"Well, shit, bambolina. If Nonna doesn't approve, that's it. We have to call off the engagement. You'll have to pack your shit and move out." I laugh.

"Wait… engagement? What did I miss?" Lilah asks with wide eyes.

"Nothing. There is no engagement." Maddie glares at me. "Don't give her ideas, Theo."

"There sure is," I tell Lilah. "Maddie just doesn't

know it yet." Then I turn to my girl. "Don't stress. Trust me when I say my Nonna loves everyone."

The front door swings open and we're greeted by a housekeeper. "Mr. Valentino, welcome. Mr. and Mrs. Donatello are in the sunroom."

"Thank you." I nod and walk in that direction. My grandmother favors the sunroom most of all, despite the various over-the-top options this estate offers. Entering the room, I find not only my grandparents but also my Uncle Neo and Aunt Angelica as well as my cousin Izzy.

Nonna gasps as she stands. A shaky hand hovers at her mouth and her eyes water up. "Oh my gosh, it's her," she whispers.

"Aunt Gloria, you okay?" Neo asks.

Nonna comes over and engulfs the girls in a hug. "You have no idea what a pleasure it is to meet you both," she says.

"Ah, Nonna, I'm here also. You know, your favorite grandchild." I wink at Izzy, who sends me a death glare. I'd like to say she's a spoiled princess, because she fucking is. But she's also scary as shit. That girl inherited her mother's kind of crazy for sure.

"Theo, jealousy is not a good look on you," Nonna says as she reaches over to me. I bend down to greet her with a kiss to each cheek.

"Maddie, Lilah, you remember Neo and Angelica.

This is their *spawn*, Izzy. My cousin," I introduce. "And this is my nonno—Al."

"It's nice to meet you all. Thank you so much, Mrs. Donatello, for inviting us to lunch," Maddie says quickly.

"Nonsense, child, this home is your home. You're always welcome here. Always." Nonna dabs at her eye with a tissue. I look to Neo for help. I know that she knew their mother. I just didn't think it would have this kind of effect on her.

"Lo, let's go check on the lunch in the kitchen," Aunt Angelica says, taking hold of her arm and leading her out of the room.

"Is your Nonna always that emotional?" Maddie asks me.

"More often than not." I laugh.

"Okay, you look way too sweet for the likes of *him*." Izzy shoots a thumb in my direction. "Blink once if you need rescuing. Twice if you want me to make him hurt," Izzy says to Maddie.

"Ah, what?" she replies, wide-eyed.

"Really, I can and will make him hurt if you need me to. I won't even break a sweat. Do you need rescuing?"

My girl looks from me to Izzy with a small smile. "Don't even think about it, Maddie. She's not joking. Unfortunately. So much for family loyalty, Iz," I inter-ject, leading the girls over to the sofa while not letting go of Maddie's hand as I sit down and pull her next to me.

"Oh, I'm loyal, but let's not pretend. We all know she's out of your league, Theo."

I don't argue with her, because she's right. Maddie is way out of my league. I just don't care.

After lunch, Nonna packed up a stack of leftovers for us to take home. I think we'll have enough food for the entire week at this rate.

"Your family is very..." Maddie trails off, no doubt looking for the right choice of word.

"Intense, in your face, annoying, overbearing?" I offer up.

"Loving," she says finally. "It must have been nice growing up surrounded by so many people who love you. Lilah and I just had our parents. They were both only children and their extended family members were all either dead or estranged."

Fuck, that's what they think? They don't realize they have two very large families in this city. Two families on opposing sides of each other. The Mortellos, their mother's namesake, are one of the five Italian families ruling New York, while the Petrovs are the heads of a fucking

Russian crime organization. There is no love lost between the two. I wonder if I can tell her about her Italian side and just ignore the Russian part. It's not like I'd ever let her near any of those fuckers anyway.

Before we make it home, my phone rings. It's my uncle. "Zio Neo, miss me already?" I ask.

"Like a hole in the head, TJ," he says. He's the only one who calls me that: TJ, Theo Junior. I've not allowed anyone else. And even he hardly uses the nickname he gave me.

"What do you want?" I ask.

"I forgot to mention we have New Year's plans. My place, no later than eight," he orders.

"Why the fuck do I have to be there?" I never spend New Year's with the family. Usually Matteo and I get shitfaced. Guess that won't be happening this year.

"Because I said so. Dr. Fuckface and Lola will be here. I need you around to make sure I don't accidently slit his fucking throat."

Now it all makes sense. My uncle absolutely despises his sister's husband, Doctor James. Neo hired him back before I was even born to help my Aunt Lola recover from her trauma. She was kidnapped and missing for ten years. I don't know everything that happened to her, but I have a fair idea. I know how fragile she is though. Even after all this time, she's still a little messed up. Not that anyone holds that against her.

"Fine, we'll be there." I hang up the phone right as we're pulling into the parking lot. It's late afternoon by the time we get home. I've had a few of my guys arrange for a tree and some gifts to be set up in the penthouse. I wasn't planning on Maddie and Lilah being here today, but now that they are, I'm not about to have them miss out on gifts on Christmas Day.

The aroma of cinnamon hits me as soon as we walk into the apartment. Okay, maybe the guys went a little beyond just a tree. It's like a winter fucking wonderland in here. Every square inch is decorated. Maddie gasps beside me while Lilah squeals in excitement.

"Ah, did someone break in and decorate your place, Theo?" Maddie asks, looking confused. "How could anyone do all this. We weren't even gone that long?"

"Merry Christmas," I say, kissing the side of her head. "Come on." I lead both girls farther into the room.

"Mr. Valentino, good evening." Rose, my housekeeper, comes out of fuck knows where, carrying a tray of mugs. She places everything on the coffee table. "I've left dinner in the oven warming for whenever you're ready, sir. Enjoy your evening." She walks away.

"Thank you, Rose," I call after her retreating back.

"Who's that?" Maddie whispers.

"Rose? She cooks and cleans for me." I pick up a mug of hot chocolate and hand one to Lilah, and then another to Maddie. "Now, I don't know about you ladies, but those gifts are begging to be ripped open." There are at least twenty boxes under the tree. All for my girls.

"Theo... we don't need gifts," Maddie replies nervously.

"I know you don't need them, but you have them." I walk over to the tree and pick up the first box. I know what I instructed my men to purchase, so I have a fair idea what's in the rectangular box I hand Lilah. "For you. Look, it even has your name on it."

"Thank you, Theo, but really you didn't have to get me gifts. I don't have anything for you," Lilah says quietly.

"Just open it, sweetheart," I groan. These girls really need to get used to accepting gifts.

She rips into the paper and stares wide-eyed at the white box with an apple logo on it. "Holy shit..." She covers her mouth.

"Language," Maddie scolds.

"Sorry, but really, this is a MacBook, Theo."

"I saw that ancient device you were using for your schoolwork. Figured you could use a new one." I shrug. It's not a big deal.

"Thank you." Lilah jumps up from the sofa and throws her arms around me, catching me off guard.

I'm a little frozen to the spot as I look at Maddie for help. But she just laughs. I pat Lilah's back a couple of times. What else can I do? "Don't mention it. I'm glad you like it."

Lilah steps back. "I love it." She returns to her spot on the sofa and I go to the tree, deciding it will be easier if I just bring the entire pile over to them. I scoop up everything with Lilah's name on it, placing the boxes in front of her.

Then I do the same with the rest. They're all for Maddie. While Lilah is busy ripping into the gifts, Maddie is just staring at the boxes. "What's wrong, bambolina?" I ask her.

"No one's ever done anything like this for us before. Well, besides our parents. But this… it's a lot, Theo."

"It's not even close to what I want to give you, Maddie. I want to give you the whole fucking world. And if you'll let me, I will."

"I don't need the world. I just need one thing," she says, biting her bottom lip.

"What's that?" Whatever it is, I will find a way to get it for her.

"You?" she questions.

I smile. "You already have that, bambolina, and there are no returns or refunds where I come from."

CHAPTER 19
Maddie

I'm in shock. I can't believe Theo went to so much trouble for me and Lilah. When he said *there were no returns or refunds*, I laughed. This is the first Christmas in two years where I've laughed, where I've felt joy. And it's the first Christmas since our parents died that Lilah has been so excited, ripping through gifts like she's ten years old again.

"Ah, do you guys mind if I go and set this baby up in my room?" she asks.

"Guest room. It's not yours, Lilah," I remind her. We don't live here, as much as Theo insists that we now do.

"It's yours. And go for it," Theo says, and I watch my sister run off down the hall. "You haven't opened anything." He states the obvious.

"Well, there is something I want to open, but not

here. Come on." I stand and take his hand, pulling him into his bedroom. I shut and lock the door behind me. With my hands on his chest, I shove him farther into the room. "You said I have you, right? All of you?' I ask him.

He smirks down at me. "Every fucking inch, bambolina."

"Good," I say, dropping to my knees in front of him. As my fingers undo his belt, then his button, I slowly drag his zipper down.

"Merde," he curses under his breath as his heated gaze runs through me.

I tug down his pants and briefs, freeing his already hard cock. Tilting my head, I look up at him. "Are you always hard? Like constantly ready to go?" I ask him.

"Ever since I first saw you."

My hand wraps around his shaft, pumping slowly up and down. I lean in and lick up the under-side of his cock, right along the pulsing vein, before swirling my tongue around his tip, lapping up the precum that's leaking out of him.

"Fuck, bambolina. It's taking all of my fucking restraint to let you have this control and not fuck your face right now," he groans.

My whole body shivers. I don't know what it is, but I want to be used by him. Owned by him. That thought shocks me. Because while I want to be owned by him in the bedroom, I also want to be independent outside of it. I want to make my own rules, live my own life. And I'm not sure one can be achieved without compromising the other.

Closing my lips around him, I take him as far back as I can, which certainly isn't all of him. So I wrap my hand around the base of his cock, pumping as I hollow out my cheeks, and suck while sliding him in and out.

"Fuck. Your mouth is fucking perfect," he hisses. Taking a fistful of my hair, he holds me back. I know I'm not good at giving head. I've only done it on the odd occasion, and each time, the guy I'm with gets impatient and pulls me back up.

I want to please Theo though. I want to give him the mind-blowing kind of pleasure he gave me last night. Releasing his cock from my mouth, I peer up at him, "Show me," I tell him.

"Show you what?"

"Show me how you want to fuck my face…"

His lips tilt up at the corners. His hands palm each side of my face as his thumb traces along my bottom lip. "So fucking perfect. You are so goddamn perfect. You're going to take every inch of me down this little throat of yours, bambolina," he commands.

My eyes widen because he can't be serious. It's not physically possible to fit all of him. It's not my fault he's so big.

"Trust me, relax and open that mouth." As soon as my lips part, he slides his cock in slowly. "Take a breath and hold it," he tells me. When I do as he instructs, he continues to shove his cock into my throat. And I can't help but choke around it. I start to panic when he pulls back out. "Relax, bambolina, you can do this," he says while caressing my face.

Taking a deep breath, I nod my head. *I can do this.* He repeats the motion, gradually sliding into the back of my throat again, and I don't panic as much this time. Closing my eyes, I try to focus on him. On his taste. His smell. Everything that is Theo.

"Open your eyes," he says in a deep, husky voice. "I want to see your eyes when I come down your throat." He starts to pull away. "Breathe through your nose, Maddie. I'm not stopping if you fucking pass out, and I really don't want you drowning on my cum."

I groan around his cock. Something about his bossy tone goes straight to my core, igniting a fire inside me. My hands grab hold of his thighs as he picks up his speed. Pumping in and out of my mouth. Not holding anything back now. He is fucking my face.

"Fuck, Jesus Christ, Maddie, I'm going to come and you're going to swallow every last fucking drop." That's when I feel the warm spurts of his seed fill my mouth. I do my best to swallow it all, but there's so much that some of it drips down my cheeks. When he's finished, he leans down and picks me up from the floor. "How'd I get so lucky to get you?" he whispers, tugging his pants upward before adjusting the zipper.

"Serendipity?" I offer.

"Fate, you were fucking made for me. An angel sent to earth for me."

I laugh at that. "We both know God isn't sending men like you angels, Theo."

"Men like me?" he asks.

"You're a gangster. You do bad things. Do you really think God rewards people who do bad things?"

"Who says getting an angel like you is a reward?" he asks.

I frown. Am I a nuisance to him? Am I more trouble than I'm worth? Last night has been on my mind all day... what he did to get me out of that situation I got myself into.

"Don't look like that, bambolina. What I meant is, while you are every bit a reward here on earth, I'm stuck with the knowledge that we're headed to very different places in the next life. While you're going up, I'm going down. And I don't fucking like the idea of spending eternity without you."

"You barely know me, Theo. Who knows? Maybe I've done some bad things in my life that have gotten me kicked out of heaven too."

"Oh yeah? Like what? Did you return a library book late or something?"

"No, I killed my parents," I whisper.

CHAPTER 20

Theo

"I killed my parents." Maddie's words make me freeze. What the fuck does she mean she killed her parents?

"What?" I ask her. I must have heard her wrong.

"I killed them," she repeats.

"How?" I prod her. I honestly wouldn't care if she killed the fucking Pope. She's still my perfect bambolina, no matter what sins she's committed.

"It was my fault. I was away at college. I was homesick and begged them to come and see me. Begged them to make the three-hour drive to visit me." Tears run down her face. I use my thumbs to wipe them away. "When they didn't show up that night, I hated them. I thought they just didn't care. That they weren't coming. I found out the next morning that they died in a car accident while they were on their way to me."

"Maddie, that wasn't your fault. You didn't kill them." I wrap my arms around her and hold her as tight as I can.

"I might not have physically caused the crash, but it was my fault. If I didn't make them come to visit me, they would have been at home. They wouldn't have been on the road with that drunk driver."

"What happened to him?" I ask her, curious.

"Huh?"

"What happened to the drunk driver?"

"He died as well. Nikolai Petrov. I'll never forget his name. He died on impact. Like my dad. My mom… she died on the way to the hospital."

"Fuck," I curse, releasing her to pull out my phone and call my father. Maddie looks at me like I've grown a second head as I pace up and down while waiting for him to answer.

"Theo, now really isn't a good time. I'm still trying to clean up that little incident of yours from last night."

"Nikolai Petrov, who is he?" I ask.

"He was Alexei's brother. He died a few years back from what I hear. Why?"

"He was the driver—the one who killed Maddie's parents. They put a hit out on their own fucking family," I hiss.

"Theo, calm down. I'll dig around and find out if the Petrovs know anything about the girls. If they do, it's unlikely they'd still be alive."

"I'll kill every last fucking one of them. Wipe the fucking bloodline clean."

"Don't do anything stupid, Theo. That's a fucking order. Wait until I look into it."

"Fine," I grit out and hang up.

"Theo, what's going on?" Maddie asks.

"Ah, shit. Maddie, I'm sorry." I walk up and wrap my arms around her. Lifting her off her feet, I sit on the bed with her on my lap. "Your parents... they weren't Smiths, Maddie. They were members of the criminal underground..." I begin to tell her.

"I know," she says.

"I'm—wait? You know?"

"My parents never lied to us, Theo. They told us who they used to be, what types of people their families were, and that if we were ever to run into anyone from that world, we needed to run."

"Then why didn't you? Why didn't you run when you met me?"

"Because I heard my parents arguing once. The name Theo Valentino came up a lot in that argument. My mom wanted to go to him for help and my father refused to let her." She shrugs. "I mean, my mom obviously trusted the man, so I figured maybe I could too. And maybe enough time passed that your family wouldn't recognize us."

"My dad and Neo knew right away, Maddie. My grandmother also."

"We should probably go. I should take Lilah and run, like I should have done after my parents died."

"You're not running. I'm not going to let anything happen to you. Either of you." I hold her tighter. We sit there in silence for what seems like minutes but I know is at least an hour. "We should eat dinner," I whisper into her hair.

"I'm not hungry," she murmurs into my chest.

"We need to feed Lilah at least."

"She's sixteen, Theo, not ten. She's capable of fetching her own food." She laughs.

"She's a child. I'll get her a plate of something and take it to her." Lifting Maddie up a second time, I place her on the bed and tuck the blanket around her.

"You're going to spoil her," Maddie says.

"Well, at least she lets me." I laugh. After giving Lilah a plate of food and a bottle of water, I head into the living room and pick up all the gift boxes Maddie didn't open. I then make my way back to the bedroom and dump the boxes on the bed. "You didn't open your presents, bambolina."

"Mmm, pretty sure I unwrapped the best thing already." She smiles and her eyes light up.

I can't help but adjust myself in my pants at the mention of her mouth around my cock. "And you can unwrap that one anytime you want. But, right now, I want you to open these."

Maddie rolls her eyes. "It's not that I'm not grateful, Theo, but this is too much. I feel bad that I don't have anything for you."

"Well, there is something you can give me."

"What?"

"New Year's Eve, I want you to say yes to everything on that day. Every answer that comes out of your mouth will be a yes."

"Mmm, what if you ask me something weird like to run nude through Times Square, or to have a threesome with you and some random guy?"

"Yeah, that's never fucking happening. Ever!" I growl. "That pussy of yours is now mine, bambolina. You are mine and I'm not sharing you with anyone."

"I'll think about it," she says, picking up the closest gift and ripping it open.

It's a box of candy hearts. "You got me candy?" She smiles.

"Read them," I instruct her. The inscription on each says: *TV + MS*.

"Oh my gosh, how did you get these?" she says, popping one into her mouth. She then picks up her phone and takes a photo before tapping at the screen.

"Who are you messaging?"

"Gia. She'd never believe that you could be so sweet if I don't show her the evidence."

"I'm not sweet, Maddie."

"Well, I disagree. You got me heart candies, Theo. What's sweeter than that?"

"You."

She rolls her eyes again before she rips into the next box, and the next, and then the next. There's a theme to the gifts I picked out. They all make clear my claim on her. Right down to the fake tattoo sticker that reads: *property of Theo Valentino.*

"This is not going on my skin, Theo." Maddie laughs when she plucks the sticker sheet out of the box.

"Why not?" I pout. I really did want to see that fake tattoo on her.

"One, I'm no one's property. And, two, if I wanted your name tattooed on me, I'd go to a shop and get it done for real."

"Over my dead fucking body," I growl, tackling her down onto the bed. Holding her hands above her head, I make sure my voice is steady. Clear. "The only person who will mark your body is me, bambolina. No other man will ever touch this beautiful skin of yours." I straddle her legs, sit up, and start unbuttoning my shirt.

"Okay," she breathes out. Her compliance almost has me questioning her. Why is she being so submissive now? Then I see where her eyes are looking. Right at my fucking crotch, my hard-on extremely noticeable through the fabric of my dress pants.

"See something you want, bambolina?" I ask her.

"Uh-huh." She nods her head while licking her lips.

"Fuck." I work faster at stripping out of my

clothes, having to stand to lose my pants. I drag her to the end of the bed. Lifting her dress over her head, I reach around and unclip her bra before removing her panties. "I think you should just give up on wearing underwear, Maddie. I plan on having you out of them more often than you'll be in them."

"Maybe," she says as she spreads her thighs, showing me exactly how ready for me she is.

I lean down and swipe my fingers through her wet folds, inserting one inside her sweet cunt and collecting her juices. My mouth closes around one of her nipples. Withdrawing my fingers from her cunt, I slide them farther back, poking at her other hole. Maddie freezes at my touch.

"This ass is mine too, Maddie. Make no mistake about that," I grunt around her nipple, biting down gently on the soft flesh. The motion has her hips arching off the bed.

While she's distracted by that pleasure, I insert a finger into her asshole. "Oh, fuck. Theo."

"That's exactly what I plan to do," I say as I slowly pump my finger in and out. She's squirming beneath me as I lavish her tits with attention while fucking her ass with my finger.

"Please," she pleads.

"Please what, Maddie?"

"I need you. Inside me. Now," she hisses.

She whimpers when I withdraw my finger to flip her over. I have her positioned on all fours. Lining my cock up with the entrance of her pussy, I bury myself inside her in one thrust. Then I insert my finger back into her ass and fuck both her holes. *Relentlessly*. Her moans and cries and pleas for me are fucking music to my ears.

She loves everything I have to give her. I don't hold back, adding another finger to her ass. She freezes, her cunt milking my cock as the orgasm takes over her body. My own orgasm is close behind. I don't pull out. I coat her walls with my seed, just like I wanted to last night, keeping my cock buried inside her until all of her aftershocks are finished. Until I'm absolutely drained of cum.

CHAPTER 21
Maddie

I'm woken by someone peppering kisses all over my face. I swat my hand out, slapping at the intrusion. "Just a few more minutes," I mumble.

"Doc is here, bambolina. I thought you might want to talk to him before he starts Lilah's treatment."

Shit… I shoot up in the bed. "What time is it?"

"A bit after ten."

"Why didn't you wake me sooner?" I shove the blankets away, and Theo stands back.

"What the fuck?" he says, looking me up and down. I glance at myself to see what he's staring at. My naked body. Covered in bite marks and fingerprints.

"Huh, did I forget to mention I bruise easily?" I ask him.

"Are you okay? Did I... did I hurt you?" His question is barely above a whisper. He sounds so unsure.

"Theo, stop looking at me like that. You didn't do anything I didn't want. So don't even think about going soft on me now."

"Are you sure?"

"Positive." I smile. I push myself off the bed and reach up on my tiptoes to kiss him. "I liked every minute of it." I wink before heading to the bathroom. Showering as quickly as I possibly can, I walk back into the bedroom and find Theo sitting on the bed waiting for me. He has a dress laid out beside him. A dress that isn't mine. "Where did that come from?"

"The closet," he says.

"I'm not wearing something that belonged to any of your ex-girlfriends or bimbos, Theo."

"I don't have any ex-girlfriends, Maddie, and no bimbo has ever entered this apartment. I bought this for you."

"Why?" I ask, picking up the dress. It's a royal-blue color with long sleeves and a wrap-around body.

"Why not?" he questions back.

Shit, what am I supposed to say to that? Why not? "Because I'm not your kept woman. I refuse to be kept."

"Well, I'm keeping you anyway. But you're not kept in the sense you're implying."

I glare at him. I'm at a loss for words. I want to argue that he can't keep me. But, at the same time, I want nothing more than to be *his* forever. What the hell is wrong with me? I'm not this girl. The one who gets blinded by cock. Sure, his is super nice, probably the best-looking one I've ever seen, and he most certainly knows how to use it. But I will not be cock-blinded.

"Bambolina, if you keep thinking about my cock, I'm going to have to pull it out and fuck you with it. Again."

My mouth opens wide. "How did you know I was thinking about it?"

"The fact that your eyes are honed in on my crotch. Your cheeks are red. Your breathing has picked up, and I can see the pulse in your neck beating faster."

"Oh." That's it... That's all of the response I have for that.

"Maddie, get dressed. It's not easy for me to hold back when it comes to you."

I quickly dig out a pair of panties and a bra from my bag that's sitting in the corner of the room. Theo wanted me to unpack it. I haven't... yet. Once I'm dressed, he takes my hand, guiding me into his theater room where Lilah is chatting up a storm with the doctor.

"Are you sure he's as good as you say he is? He's

really young." I turn to Theo, keeping my peripheral vision locked on the man in question.

"You think I'd bring him around if he wasn't the best?"

"Well, probably not," I answer.

"Definitely not," he corrects. "Doc, are we all set up?" Theo asks him.

"Yep, we're good to get started." The doctor looks at me. "I reviewed Lilah's charts from the hospital. Do you have any questions?"

"Um, no, I don't think so." I maneuver towards my sister and take a seat beside her. "Lilah, are you sure you're okay with doing this here?"

"Are you kidding? This is way better than being stuck in that hospital. Thank you, Theo," she says, craning her neck to look at him.

"Sure, do you need anything? Want some snacks or something?" he asks her.

"Um, some water?" Lilah answers.

"I'll be right back." Theo nods to the doctor and walks out. Something seems off with him. I'm not sure what it is though.

"I'm just going to get a coffee. Are you okay?" I ask Lilah again.

"I'm fine. We can get started whenever you're ready, Doc." Lilah straightens the arm now resting on a wedge cushion.

I find Theo in the kitchen making coffee. "Is everything okay?" I ask him.

"Everything's fine. Why wouldn't it be?" He doesn't turn around and look at me like he usually would.

"It's okay if you're not, you know. You don't have to be okay all the time, Theo," I say calmly.

"Yes, I do. I don't have a choice. It's my responsibility to make sure everything runs smoothly, to make sure everyone is safe. I fix things, Maddie. That's what I do. It's what I'm good at. And as much as I want to fucking fix Lilah for you, for her, there's not a damn fucking thing I can do about it. So am I okay? No, I'm not. I don't like when things are out of my fucking control. Unless you've reconsidered your stance on a black market kidney. Because *that* I could actually fucking do," he says, his chest heaving up and down.

"It's okay. I don't expect you to fix her, Theo. I don't expect you to do anything for us. What you're doing, it's already more than I could ever ask for."

"How do you handle it?"

"I don't handle it. I cry in the shower just about every night. And I fake it. Because I don't want to burden her with my worries. My worry that she's going to die and I'll be alone in this world. Without any family."

Theo's arms enclose around me. "You will never be alone, Maddie. And she's not dying. There are still at least fifty guys Doc has yet to test. We will find a match."

"It's okay if you don't. This isn't on you, Theo." He doesn't say anything, but he does kiss my forehead before he goes back to making coffee. "I can make that you know," I offer.

"Not a fucking chance. You're clearly great at many things, Maddie, but you make shit coffee." He laughs.

"What? But you came into Grind The Bean every day for almost two weeks and demanded I make your coffee. Why would you do that if you didn't like it?"

"Because I like you." He lifts a shoulder like it makes perfect sense. And perhaps in his messed-up head, it does.

I've been watching reruns of *The Vampire Diaries* with Lilah for the last two hours while Theo works in his office. The doctor pops his head in every fifteen minutes to check on her, which is way more often than she ever got checked on in the hospital. A few minutes into the latest episode, Theo walks into the theater room and holds his phone out to me. "You have a call," he grunts.

I take the phone and he turns around, walking back out. "Hello?"

"Oh my god, Maddie, where the hell are you? Do you know how worried I've been all morning? Why haven't you been answering my calls?" Gia's voice screeches through the receiver. I have to pull the phone away from my ear so I don't go deaf.

"Shit, I'm sorry, Gia. I forgot to tell you. We're at Theo's place."

"Obviously. Lilah's with you? How is she getting to the hospital today?"

"Ah, she's doing her treatment here. Theo had the doctor come and set it up in his apartment. I should have called you. It's just... I woke up late, then I got sucked into the whole Stefan versus Damon debate with Lilah. You know she really does have a thing for a bad boy. I'm a little concerned about her choices." I laugh.

"Seems like it runs in the family," Gia sasses. "I'm so glad you're okay, but don't ever make me worry like that again. I don't like it."

"I won't. Promise."

"So, how long are you holing up in lover boy's place?"

"Ah, I'm not sure."

"Is there something you're not telling me, Maddie? You didn't run off to Vegas and get married or anything, did you?"

"No, you know when I get married, you'll be standing up there with me."

"Good, because I haven't been dieting my whole life to not wear that bridesmaid dress."

I laugh. Gia and I used to always talk about our weddings. We had everything planned, down to the china—well, everything but the grooms. "I love you," I tell her.

"You too. I gotta go, but call me. Text me, whatever." She hangs up.

"I'll be back, Lilah. I'm just going to give Theo his phone back." I find him sitting behind a large mahogany desk. I've not been into his office yet. Standing on the threshold, I knock on the open door and his head pops up, his gaze moving from his computer screen to me.

"Everything okay?" he asks as he drops his gaze again.

"Yep. Sorry that she called your phone," I say, walking into the room before I place his cell down in front of him.

"It's fine."

"Is there anything I can do?" I ask him. I don't know why he's stressed, what he's worried about, but I want to help. I want to do anything I can to help. I don't like seeing him look so lost. So out of sorts.

He pushes his chair away from the desk. "Come here," he says, crooking his index finger at me. I walk around and he pulls me into his lap. He brings one hand up to the top of my head and strokes the hair away from my face, tucking it behind my ear before he twirls his finger around the bottom of the strands. "You being here is helping," he says, leaning his forehead against mine.

"Want to talk about it? Whatever is bothering you?"

"I can't. There are some things in my job I can't talk to you about, Maddie. It's for your own safety. The less you know, the better."

I wrap my arms around his neck, bring my lips to his, and kiss him softly. "I'm sorry if I've caused you trouble. I really didn't know what happened at that club," I say. We haven't talked about that night and I feel like it's the elephant in the room most of the time.

"I know."

"Are you getting a lot of backlash? Are you in danger, Theo?" I ask him, not really wanting to know the answer.

"Are you worried about me, bambolina?" He grins, easily evading my question with one of his own. I've noticed he does that a lot.

"I am. It would be cruel for you to barge yourself into my life only to end up gone."

"I'm not going anywhere."

"You can't be so sure of that."

"I promise you I will always do everything in my power to come home. No matter what happens, I don't ever plan on being the one who ends up in the ground."

I know it's not possible for him to make such a promise. I know from the very few stories our parents told us about the mafia that it's not a safe life. It's why they left. Why they changed their names. Lived a different life. "Have you ever thought about leaving?"

"No. There's only one way out, Maddie, and it's not one I'm ready for."

I think of my parents. They got out. They left. I know it caught up with them eventually, but they had twenty years of a good, happy, *normal* life. Sure, we had struggles like every other middle-class family in Brooklyn. But we were together.

"I'm sorry that you had to see what you saw that night. I will do my best to keep you away from any situation like that again," he says.

"Am I a horrible person? I mean, I should be frightened, right? I shouldn't be so willingly staying here with my little sister after what you did. But I'm not scared of you. I'm scared of not having you. And that's crazy because we barely know each other."

"I think I know you plenty well enough." His gaze heats as he looks me up and down. "I've never wanted anyone as much as I want you," he says.

"What about when the lust fades? What's going to happen when you decide you've had enough of me?"

"That's not ever going to happen," he promises. Cupping my cheeks in his hands, he leans in, claiming my mouth with his own. His tongue slides out and parts my lips, seeking entrance, which of course my greedy body gives him without a fight. I don't hear the footsteps and the voices that proceed down the hall, but Theo pulls away from me, groaning. "Remind me I can't shoot my own brothers. My mother wouldn't like it," he whispers, right before three men walk through the door of his office.

"Wh—oh, hey, Maddie. Good to see you. Didn't know you'd be here." Matteo smiles at me.

"Yes you did, asshole. What the fuck are you all doing here?"

"Pops sent us back. Apparently we're to stay here with you until he and Ma return from Canada," Romeo says, sitting down on one of the sofas in the room.

"Why would he send you back early?" Theo asks.

"Beats me, but I'm not complaining. I'm hungry. Don't worry, bro, I know where you keep the good snacks." Luca walks out of the room, heading for the pantry I'm assuming.

"Ah, I should go check on Lilah. Do you need anything?" I ask Theo as I push to my feet.

"Yes, I do," he groans, adjusting himself in his trousers. My lips tip up at one side, trying not to laugh at his distress.

"Sorry," I whisper before walking out.

CHAPTER 22
Theo

"**R**omeo, get up and shut the door," I tell my younger brother, who is sprawled out on my sofa with his fucking feet up on the coffee table. He groans but follows the order anyway. "What the fuck are you all really doing here?" I direct my question to Matteo, who falls into one of the chairs opposite my desk.

"You apparently went nuts and shot up Club S. We're here to make sure you're not alone when those Gambino fuckers come for your ass." He shrugs.

"I'm not worried about them coming for me," I lie. There's not a chance in hell they're not going to seek retribution for what I did. It's why I insisted Maddie and Lilah stay here. I know whenever they take a shot at me, it won't be in this building. It'll be somewhere public. The crazy bastards love to make a scene. And killing me would be their biggest one yet.

"Sure you're not. What's to worry about?" Romeo rolls his eyes as he helps himself to my fucking whiskey.

"Romeo, don't you have a study partner to go hang out with or something?" I ask him.

"Nope," he says, sitting back on the sofa. He takes his phone out of his pocket and starts messaging someone.

"What's the plan, boss?" Matteo asks.

"Wait it out, let them try to come at me. I've got a bigger issue to deal with right now than the Gambino family."

"Like what? Domestic life not cracking up to what Pops tries to tell us it is?" Matteo laughs.

"Need I remind you I'm not the one who's married here? How is Savvy anyway?" I smirk when all he does is groan. "The Petrovs killed Maddie's parents," I tell both Romeo and Matteo, a little thankful that Luca isn't within earshot. Out of the four of us, he's the most reckless and I don't need him running out and doing something fucking stupid.

"How do you know?"

"Maddie told me. She knows who her parents were. Well, she knows whatever version they told her anyway. The drunk driver who hit them was a Petrov. What I don't understand is, if they knew about Lana and Alexei, why did they leave the girls alive. It's not like the Russians to leave anyone breathing." My fists clench at the thought of anyone coming after Maddie or Lilah.

"Maybe they don't know about them? Could it have been a coincidence?"

"Coincidences don't happen in this world of ours, Matteo."

"You're right. What does Pops say to do?" Romeo asks.

"To sit tight and wait for further info. I don't want either of you repeating this threat to Maddie or Lilah. They have enough to worry about without being scared for their lives."

"What about the Mortellos? You think they know about the girls? I don't see how they'd leave them unprotected," Matteo counters.

The Mortellos are close friends of ours. "I doubt they know they even exist," I answer. They're good people. They're not likely to put a hit out on their own blood. Nic Mortello is the current head of the family, and if I'm right, I'd say he's a second cousin to Maddie and Lilah. He's also fiercely passionate about family.

"Well, since we're all stuck here with your pleasant ass, I'm going to hit the gym, then shower and find a bed." Romeo stands, stretching his arms above his head.

"Lilah's in the first guest room. You three can find others," I tell him.

"What? Why does she get the best room? I'm your

favorite brother," he sulks.

"I like her better." I smile.

"Ass," he mumbles as he walks out.

Matteo stares at me. I can see the million questions running across his face—questions he wants to ask now that we're alone. There is only so much we tell the other two. They're still way too fucking young to be mixed up in this mess. As long as I can keep them out of it, I will. "What are you really planning, Theo?" he finally spits out.

"I have a sit down with Harry Gambino tomorrow night," I tell him.

"Like fuck you do. You go into that sit down and you're not walking out. Don't be fucking stupid," he seethes.

"I don't have a fucking choice. I made this mess, and if it meant protecting Maddie, I'd fucking do it again too."

"I'm the spare, Theo. I don't ever want to be the fucking heir. You're not allowed to die and put that shit on me."

I know he doesn't mean it the way he says it. We've always joked around, saying that he's the spare while I'm the heir. He's never once wanted my role in the family, so maybe a part of him isn't joking about it now. "I'm not planning on dying. You can't get rid of me that easily."

"Fine, I'm coming with you," he says.

"No, I need you to stay here with Maddie and

Lilah. You're the person I trust most in this world to keep them safe, Matteo. And right now, I value their lives far more than my own."

Matteo doesn't say anything. Instead, he stands, walks out, and slams the door. I know he doesn't like what I'm planning; he doesn't want to be the one left behind at home while I'm out meeting with someone who no doubt wants to put a bullet between my eyes.

After another hour of staring at the building plans and the interior of the restaurant where I'm expected to meet Old Man Gambino, I finally feel like I know all the entrances, all the vantage points in the room. I'm not going in blind. I will know how to get my ass out of that place if need be. Maybe I should tell Uncle Neo, my Pops even. But I don't because I know if I do, they'll stop me from going. And if I don't show up, it'd just be another big *fuck you* from the Valentinos to the Gambinos.

It's been too long since I set my eyes on Maddie. Shutting down my computer, I head out in search of her, stopping at the theater room first. Doc left about ten minutes ago. He popped his head in and said he'd be back in two days. I don't find Maddie there, though. What I do find is Luca and Lilah looking way more friendly than they should. They're watching some stupid vampire show, surrounded by snacks and soft drinks. My brother says something I don't hear, making Lilah laugh.

"Luca," I yell out over the noise of the speakers. His head turns in my direction. "A word. Now!" I walk back out of the room and wait just outside the door. When he steps into the hall, I shove him against the wall. "What the fuck do you think you're doing?" I growl in his face.

"Woah, what?" He holds up his hands.

"Stay the fuck away from Lilah. She's fucking sixteen for god's sake." I shove him again.

"Ah, yeah, that's not what this is, Theo. Jesus, what do you take me for?"

"She's a kid, Luca. Don't fucking forget that." I leave him standing there, making my way to the other side of the apartment in search of Maddie. She's the one thing that gives me peace lately. It terrifies me just how much I need her. I find Romeo in the living room eating a bowl of popcorn. "Clean up that mess," I tell him, pointing at the popcorn all over the floor. "Have you seen Maddie?"

"Matteo took her to the gym," he says around a mouthful of food.

"What the fuck? Why would she go to the gym with him?"

"Don't know. Don't really care."

I storm down the hallway towards my home gym.

Don't get me wrong, I trust my brothers, but the thought of Maddie in a room with any guy who isn't fucking me has me seeing red. The door slams against the wall when I enter. I see Matteo first. He's on the weight counter. Looking in the other direction, I find my target. She has a pair of headphones in her ears. Her hair is tied up in a high ponytail that swings from side to side as she runs on the treadmill. But that's not what makes me pause. It's the skintight fucking pathetic excuse for running shorts and nearly translucent sports bra she's wearing. Just about every inch of her skin is on display, glistening with a light sheen of sweat.

"Matteo, get the fuck out." My hands clench at my sides. I hear the clank of metal as he puts the bar back in its place.

He stops in front of me. "You really need to get a fucking grip on this shit, Theo, before you scare the poor girl away."

I don't acknowledge him. I know he's right. My focus stays on Maddie, on the jiggle of her ass with each step she takes. I slowly walk around the front of the treadmill. She smiles when she sees me, removing her headphones as I reach over and press the stop button on the machine. But her smile quickly disappears when she looks me up and down.

"What's wrong? What happened?" she asks.

"Strip. Now!" I command her. Taking her hand, I

lead her over to the weight counter. "Right here. Strip now, Maddie."

"What? Here? No." She folds her arms over her chest.

"No? It wasn't a fucking request. It was an order," I tell her.

"And I said no." She takes a step, as if to brush past me, and my arm snakes around her waist, pulling her back up against my chest.

"And I said strip," I growl into her ear as my hand travels down the smoothness of her stomach. Slipping beneath the Lycra shorts she is wearing, my fingers find her cunt. Wet, drenched already. With a quick tug, I yank her shorts down to her ankles. It restricts her movement as I bend her over. She catches herself on the counter. "This is fucking mine, when I want, how I want," I grunt. Kneeling behind her, I run my tongue from the front of her pussy all the way to her back hole.

She moans. "Oh, fuck, Theo." She squirms as I repeat the motion.

"Not even you will keep me from getting to this fucking pussy, bambolina. It's mine." My tongue shoves into each of her entrances, lapping up her juices.

"Fuck, Theo." She shoves her cunt harder into my face.

I can't take it anymore. I need to be inside her. Standing upright again, I free my cock and enter her from behind. "Fucking mine," I repeat over and over again as I fuck her relentlessly. Unapologetically. When I feel her walls tighten and convulse around me, I don't stop. I keep pumping in and out of her. "I want another one. You will come again for me, bambolina." I slap her right ass cheek and I feel her flood my cock.

She fucking loves it rough. Hard. Fast. We're perfectly synched in our movements. A perfect fucking match. The next time I feel her body tense, her inner walls gripping my cock harder, I let myself fall over the cliff of ecstasy with her. Emptying myself inside her. Once I've caught my breath, I pull out and pick her up before walking into the adjoining bathroom and turning the shower on. "How many showers do you have in this place?" she asks.

"Five," I answer, placing her on her feet. She toes her shoes off and then kicks the rolled-down shorts aside.

When the water is warm enough for my liking, I silently remove her sports bra, bend down, and slip off her socks. I then undress myself, tugging her under the stream. I remove the hair tie from her hair and watch as the water cascades over every inch of her skin. I reach behind her for the shampoo, massaging it into her scalp, before I tip her head back and rinse the suds away. She doesn't say anything. I pick up the loofah and proceed to wash every inch of her skin, smiling as I kneel down and see my cum leaking out of her cunt.

"Fuck, you make me so fucking crazy, Maddie. I lose my goddamn mind around you," I tell her.

"I like that you do."

"Did I hurt you?" I ask, observing the marks still coloring her body.

"Despite what you think, Theo, I'm here because I want to be. Not because you think you're forcing me to be. Because, trust me, if I really wanted out of this apartment, you wouldn't be able to stop me."

"I'll give you anything you ever ask for, Maddie, but freedom from me—yeah, that's never going to happen. If you run, I will follow you. I will find you and I will bring you right back here. Where you fucking belong."

CHAPTER 23

Maddie

Theo says I belong here, but all day I've felt a little out of place. The apartment is busy. His brothers are still here. Not that they aren't anything but polite to me and Lilah, but it's a little strange being around all of them. Theo and Matteo have been on edge with each other all day. I've been trying to stay out of the way, spending time with my sister in the bedroom she's claimed.

It's almost dinner time and Theo is in the kitchen cooking carbonara. I'm sitting at the counter, admiring the work of art that he is. I did offer to help but he quickly declined. He says my place in the world is next to him, just not when he's in the kitchen. I didn't take too much offense to that. I was kind of relieved actually. I hate cooking.

"Romeo, set an extra plate for dinner," Theo tells his brother as he deposits some salad and bread into serving bowls. It's very domesticated. I thought he would have had Rose come in daily to do his bidding. But all of the Valentino boys seem to be more than capable of taking care of themselves. I guess they have their mother to thank for that.

"Are you expecting someone else?" I ask Theo, unsure if I really have it in me to be around anyone else.

"Ah, yeah, I invited Gia. Thought you could hang out with her tonight," he says casually.

"You sick of me already? You want me out of your hair tonight?" I tease.

"I could never be sick of you. There is nothing I want more than to hang out with you, bambolina. But I gotta go out for a bit. It's a work thing."

"Okay, where are you going?" I have a right to ask that, don't I? I don't even care if I sound needy. It's his own damn fault for making me this way.

"Ah, just out. Don't worry about it," he says, walking around the counter. He kisses my forehead when the beeping sound of the elevator rings out through the apartment. "That's Gia," he announces, going back to prepping food.

I try to shove down the panic that's taking over me. Whatever he's doing tonight, it's not safe. If it were, he'd tell me about it. The thing about being told *not to worry* about something is that it's like flashing a neon sign that reads: *you should be very worried.*

Plastering on a fake smile, I go and meet Gia in the living room. She's eyeing up Matteo as he walks out of the gym. "He's married, Gia. Forget it." I chuckle as her head leans back to follow his form down the hall.

"Of course he is." She sighs before throwing her arms around me. "Jesus, I missed your face. We are not allowed to go two whole days with no contact ever again." She tightens her grip.

I cough with the added pressure to my lungs. "G, let up. You're going to break me in half." I laugh.

She steps back, her eyes traveling up and down. "What's wrong? What did he do?"

"Nothing—nothing's wrong," I lie.

"Dinner's ready," Theo calls out from behind me, saving me from the interrogation I can see on the tip of my best friend's tongue.

Once everyone is seated for dinner, I look around the table. All of the Valentino boys are larger than life. Then there's me, Gia, and Lilah. I smile. I like this. It's nice to be around a family like the Valentinos. My mind drifts to my parents again as I wonder what my dad would say if he was watching us now. He'd probably kill Theo for one. My mom would like him though. She'd see the way he treats me like I'm some rare, precious stone he's acquired. I wouldn't be surprised if he hasn't already thought about locking me up in a safe house. With four impenetrable walls. I wonder how secure this apartment of his really is. I look around the room. I don't see cameras. Though I don't doubt there're some hidden somewhere.

"What are you looking for?" Theo asks next to me.

"Wondering where all the cameras are hidden." I continue scanning the space.

"What makes you think I have cameras hiding?" Theo asks with a raised brow.

"Because you're a control freak," I answer.

Luca and Romeo laugh. "She has you there, bro," they both say at the same time.

"That's really creepy," I tell them.

"We know." Again, the response is said in unison.

I look to Theo and he just shrugs. "I'd say you get used to it, but you never fucking do."

"What are your plans for tonight?" My question is directed at the twins and Matteo, who are sitting on the opposite side of the table from us.

"We should hit the town, find some fresh meat," Luca says to Romeo.

"Pass," his twin replies.

"Come on, you never want to go out anymore."

"It's getting old." Romeo shrugs.

"What? How can it get fucking old?" Luca looks at his brother like he's lost his mind.

Theo slams his hand on the table, causing me to jump in my seat. "Luca. I will not have you speaking like that at my fucking table. Watch your goddamn mouth. There's a fucking child here," he reprimands.

Lilah laughs. "Don't worry, Theo, I know all about the birds and the bees. I'm not a virgin you know."

I knew this already. She's almost seventeen, so it's no big shock. She had a boyfriend a few months back; he disappeared as quickly as he came.

"What the fuck? Yes, you are," Theo says, pointing his fork at her.

"Ah, I don't think that's how it works, Theo." I place my hand over his.

"You knew?"

"Well, yeah, she is my sister." I gesture to my own chest, to further emphasize that she's mine. Not his.

"Well, now she's my sister too, so good luck to any motherfucker who thinks they can get within ten feet of her," he grunts.

"Okay, well, thanks for dinner, Theo. Lilah and I will clean up."

"No, Romeo and Luca will do it," he counters.

"Thanks, Theo, you're the best." Lilah flashes him an innocent smile and attempts to leave the table.

"Not so fast. You can help. You're not here to be waited on hand and foot, Lilah," I remind her. Theo groans beside me but I ignore him, giving my sister my best *don't even try me* look. I turn back to Theo. "I need a word with you." Not waiting for him, I walk into his bedroom. I know he'll follow.

A few seconds later he walks in and shuts the door. "What's wrong?" he asks.

"You have to stop spoiling Lilah. She's almost seventeen, Theo, not a little kid. And second, I want to know if you're coming back tonight?"

"Of course I plan on coming back." He *plans on coming back*. Not that he is. One thing I've noticed about Theo is that he's very deliberate with his words. Never says anything he doesn't fully mean or believe.

"*Plan to* isn't good enough, Theo. Are you going to be coming back?"

"I can't make you promises like that, Maddie. You know I can't." He sits down on the bed. Leaning his elbows on his thighs, he drops his head and runs his fingers through his hair.

He looks so broken. So stressed. I'm sure I'm just adding to it right now. But even as I know this, I can't help myself. "Well, think about how if you go and get yourself killed, I'm probably going to find some other guy, marry him, have kids with him—all that." By the time I'm finished spewing a bunch of words I don't even mean, Theo has me pinned up against the wall. Caging me in with his arms.

"There will never fucking be another man for you, Maddie. You are mine." He slams his lips down onto mine, desperate to make his claim.

I take everything that he gives. I pull away and

my eyes lock with his. "Don't break my heart, Theo," I whisper.

"I'll be back as soon as I can, bambolina. And when I do come home, I want to find you naked and waiting in my bed."

"Mmm, but if you take too long, I'm going to start without you."

"Don't touch that pussy of mine, Maddie. I will know if you do." He kisses my forehead in a sweet gesture that contradicts his crude words before walking out of the room.

It's been three hours since Theo left. Gia had a call from her mom and had to leave a few minutes ago and Lilah went to bed. Now I'm left by myself, and I have nothing to do but worry. I haven't heard from him. From Theo. I keep looking at my phone, at the blank screen. Like if I stare at it enough, I can will a text to appear. I walk into his office where I'm certain I'll find Matteo. He knows something. I know he does. He's been just as uptight as Theo all day.

I walk in right as Matteo picks up a vase and throws it against the wall. I flinch but will not cower. "What is he doing tonight, Matteo?"

"Maddie, sorry... I didn't see you there."

"What's Theo out doing?" I ask again.

Matteo peers up at me. "I can't tell you that," he says with a look that begs me not to press for details.

"It's bad. I know it is. But I just don't understand… if it's that bad, then why are you here and not with him. He shouldn't be alone. He should have someone. He can't be out there alone." I fall onto the sofa.

"He's not alone. Neo and Angelica are with him," Matteo grits out. "And I'm here because Theo values your life above his own."

I can't help the tears that stream down my cheeks. "What can I do? I have to help him. Tell me where he is, Matteo," I beg.

"Not a fucking chance. Besides the fact he'll kill me if anything were to happen to you, he'll also *kill me if anything were to happen to you.*"

"I can't… I can't." I struggle to suck in the air that my lungs so desperately need. My hands claw at my neck. I can't breathe.

"Shit. Romeo, get in here," Matteo yells as he sits in front of me. "Maddie, you need to relax. Breathe in and out slowly. You just need to relax. It's going to be okay."

"I-I can't." I shake my head, heaving in an attempt to ease the rising panic while doing the exact opposite.

"What? Holy shit, what did you do?" Romeo asks, shoving Matteo out of the way.

"Nothing! She just started freaking out."

I can hear their voices, but it sounds like everything is under water. Why does it sound like everything's underwater?

"Maddie, *bella*. You're okay. I'm going to count, and you're going to count with me, okay? Can you do that, sweetheart?" Romeo asks.

I shake my head. I can't do anything.

"Yes, you can. Repeat after me. One," he says.

"O-one."

"Good girl. Two. Say it: two," he urges.

"Two."

"Perfect, three."

"Th-th-three," I heave. By the time he gets to ten, I can breathe again. My heart rate is slowing and the panic is subsiding. "Thank you," I whisper.

"Anytime. It's just a panic attack. You're okay. We're not going to let anything happen to you, okay," Romeo promises.

"It's not me I'm worried about." I look at Matteo.

"What's she talking about?" Romeo asks his brother.

"She's worried about Theo. He had to go do something." Matteo tries to shrug it off.

"What kind of fucking suicide mission is he on? Because if all of us are here and none of us are there, it's because he's trying to be a martyr and protect us." Romeo's words represent everything that is Theo. He'd never put his brothers in jeopardy.

"He's fine. He is with Uncle Neo and Aunt Angel-ica." Matteo evades the question.

I need a drink. Pushing to my knees, then my feet, I walk over to the wet bar and pour myself a shot of Theo's whiskey. Downing it in one go, I pour another shot and repeat the process. The burn is a welcoming distraction. "If he doesn't come back tonight, I will never forgive you," I tell Matteo. I know my anger is not towards him, but right now, I need someone to blame and he's the closest target.

"He'll be back," Matteo says.

"I hope so. I'm not... I can't... We've only just started." I walk out of the office and head to Theo's bedroom. Turning the shower on, I strip out of my clothes, drop to the tiled floor, and let the tears fall.

CHAPTER 24

Theo

S itting in my car, I'm scoping out the restaurant where I'm scheduled to meet with the head of the Gambino family while sending up a little prayer that I actually make it out of here alive. I'm not ready to die. I haven't had nearly enough time with Maddie and the thought of me dying now and her moving on with some other fucker has my blood fuming. And, yes, I do know just how fucking ridiculous it is to be jealous of someone who doesn't even exist.

I know I probably should have told someone other than Matteo that I was doing this. But this is a mess of my own making. Not one I regret, but it's mine all the same. And therefore, it's my fucking responsibility to clean the shit up. I knew exactly who I was shooting on Christmas Eve. I knew before

I even stepped foot in that strip club that I'd be killing a Gambino asshole before I left.

No time like the present. I tap a hand over my torso, reminding myself of all the weapons currently strapped to my person. I want to get this shit over with so I can get back home to Maddie. I hated leaving her, hated the fear that was all over her face when I did. I wish I could say I'd never make her worry like this again, but it'd be a lie. This is the life—we live and die by it. Every action has a consequence. I just hope like fuck death isn't the consequence I'm facing tonight.

Stepping out of my car, I look up and down the street, then scan the rooftops. It's so fucking dark I can't see shit. There could be any number of snipers up on those buildings with my head already in their sights. I'm not scared of death. I've looked it in the eye more often than not lately. What I'm scared of is not living out the life I envision with Maddie. I want her to be the mother of my children. I want to show her the world.

The restaurant is empty when I push through the doors. Well, all bar the one table in the back corner with a mean-as-fuck-looking old fucker. I'm stopped two feet inside by two of his soldiers. "No guns," one of them says.

I raise an eyebrow as I slowly start to unstrap the five pistols I'm currently carrying. I was expecting this. I knew they'd strip me. The two men look at each other as I produce weapon after weapon from the underside of my suit jacket.

Yeah, fuckers, I don't need these to end any of you. My bare fucking hands will do just fine.

"Boss is ready," the second soldier says after giving me a quick, very inadequate pat down. Completely missing the fact that I still have a small pistol strapped to my left ankle, a knife on my right, and another blade sheathed against my wrist.

"Gambino." I nod as I approach the table.

"Theo, I won't lie. I'm shocked you actually came alone." His stone-cold voice gives nothing away to his mood.

"What's to say I'm alone?"

He tilts his head and looks me up and down. "You're a cocky son of a bitch—that's what."

"You got me there." I hold up my hands and smirk.

"Care to explain to me what the fuck went down in my club two nights ago?"

He already knows. He just wants to see if I'll break a sweat telling him. "Your idiot of a grandson was attempting to auction off my girl." I lift one shoulder like that's all the explanation needed.

His face reddens but he stays quiet. Stock-still. I probably shouldn't poke the bear by insulting his family members. His now-dead family members. "So you went and started a war? Is she worth it?" He raises an eyebrow.

"Did I though? Start a war?" I won't justify his question about Maddie being worth it, because she fucking is.

"Many wars have been started over women, Theo. Many of them not ending well for the lovesick couples in question."

His cryptic fucking words ignite a fire inside me. Is he threatening Maddie? Because I have no issue starting a full-blown apocalypse and putting a bullet in his head right now, matching the one I gave his fucking grandson, Samuel. So I don't answer. I tilt my head to the side and match his stare. I will not give anything away. I will not show him that he's able to get under my skin. Never show the enemy your weaknesses. Except I've already done that, haven't I? I showed the whole of fucking New York when I went in guns blazing to get Maddie.

Gambino places a folder on the table. "I've done some digging. Figured there had to be something pretty special about this girl of yours for you to do what you did." I take the folder, keeping my face void of emotion as I inspect the contents: photo after photo of Maddie, Lilah, and their parents. "It seems your girl is more than a simple struggling little thing from Brooklyn. She's a Mortello. A Petrov."

It takes everything in me not to react. "So you realize what a mistake it was for Samuel to add her to his lineup then?" I counter.

"Perhaps." He picks up his glass and takes a

measured sip of the brown liquid. "Then again, I wonder how interested the Petrovs would be in hearing of these girls' whereabouts. I gotta hand it to their parents... hiding in Brooklyn all these years with two opposing families hunting them down is no small feat." For a second time, I don't respond. I sit and wait him out. He wants something. I know he fucking does. Otherwise, I'd be dead already. "Alexei took something of great value from the Russians—something they'd do anything to get back." He slips another piece of paper over to me. It's a picture of a locket. Is the old man losing it? "I want you to find it. When you do, bring it to me."

"A locket. Why? What's its significance to you?"

"Call it sentimental," he says with a shrug.

How the fuck am I supposed to find a fucking locket? It's been twenty fucking years; that piece of jewelry could be anywhere. "What's in it for me?" I ask. *Never do anything without getting something in return.*

"The fact that the secrets surrounding your girl-friend's true identity stay just that."

"I'm not sure it really matters at this point. She's about to be a Valentino," I tell him.

A look crosses his face I can't decipher. It's not one of anger; it's more content. And it's fucking weird. "If you love the girl, you will find this locket. If it ends up in the wrong hands again, it'll start the war of all wars in this city, Theo. One where it's unlikely there will be any survivors," he says. *Again with the cryptic fucking messages.* I watch as he stands. Following his lead, I rise to my feet, fastening the button on my suit jacket. "Do we have a deal?" He holds out a palm.

Shaking his hand, I say, "If I find this locket, I'll reach out." I don't tell him that I'll give it to him, just that I'll reach out. A man's word is everything in this world. And I always make sure I'm extremely careful with the ones I use.

"Good, good." He nods his head and walks towards the back of the room. After I've collected my small arsenal, I exit the restaurant, breathing out a long sigh.

What the fuck was that?

I shouldn't question the fact that I'm walking out alive. But I fucking do. Stalking back towards the car, I freeze midstep. My hand reaches to my side as I spin around, aiming the front sight of my gun at the fucker who thought they could get the jump on me. Something hard hits the side of my head. I can't stay upright. I fall to my knees and start blindly shooting, my vision blurred as I'm kicked in the back and land face-first on the concrete.

I quickly roll over, aiming upwards. Shooting at anyone and anything. I vaguely hear a few grunts and then more gunfire rains down around me. This is it. This is how I'm going to fucking go out. Lying on the footpath of a grimy New York City street.

Yeah, not fucking likely.

I refuse. It takes all of my strength to move, and I manage to get myself to a standing position, leaning against a car. A sharp pain hits my stomach. A pain I'm all too familiar with. A fucking bullet. My hand clenches down on my abdomen as I look up, trying to hone in on the shooter. The street is surrounded by smoke. Where the fuck did all the smoke come from?

"Theo, come on, we gotta get out of here."

I almost want to fucking cry in relief at the sound of my uncle's voice. "Neo, what the fuck are you doing here?" I grunt as he ducks and takes my weight on his shoulder.

"Saving your ass apparently." He laughs. He shoves me into the back of some vehicle. "If you get blood on my seats, you're buying me a new car." This comes from Izzy as she puts foot to the metal, tires screaming as she drives like the mad woman she is.

I must have blacked out because I'm now being carried through a parking lot and into an elevator. My fucking elevator. "You shouldn't have brought me here," I grunt, my whole body aching. Neo and Izzy have their arms wrapped around one side of me as my feet drag. As much as I try to bear my own weight, all I do is stumble.

"Doc is already here," Neo says.

"Yeah, that's not why," I groan. I don't need Maddie seeing me like this. I don't want to know what this will do to her.

CHAPTER 25
Maddie

After my shower, I borrowed a white business shirt from Theo's closet. I had to roll up the sleeves quite a few times, and when I say borrowed, it's more like *stole*. Because I don't plan on giving it back to him. The silky fabric clings to my body. I don't bother putting anything on underneath it. Theo said he wanted me ready for him when he gets home, so that's what I'm going to do. I'll be ready.

I'm about to climb into bed to try to read on my kindle, to distract myself while I wait for him, when strings of fast Italian sound from inside the apartment. I run out to the main living room, my feet stopping when I see him. My whole body shakes. I'm cold and my vision blurs. Then he glances up and his eyes meet mine.

"Bambolina, it's not as bad as it looks... I promise," he says. His voice breaks me out of my shock, or panic, or whatever it was, and sends me into a rage.

"*Not as bad*. What the actual fuck, Theo? You're... you're getting blood on the carpets. What happened? Where the hell is the doctor? He should be at the hospital. Why would you bring him here?" I yell at both his uncle and his cousin, who are currently supporting his weight to keep him upright.

"Matteo, Luca, take him into the gym. Doc's set up in there," Neo instructs before he steps up to me. "Maddie, you need to calm down. He is going to be fine."

"Calm down?" I screech. "Move." I shove past him and follow behind Theo. Matteo and Luca lay him on what looks like a makeshift hospital bed. "Theo, I swear to God, you better not be fucking dying on me." I stand at his side. Tears are streaming down my face.

His eyes roam up and down my body. "Maddie, where are your fucking clothes?" he growls. "Go put some on."

"Make me!" I demand. He attempts to sit up, no doubt to do just that. To make me put fucking clothes on.

"Don't move." The doctor pushes him back down on the bed. "Boys, help me turn him. "Maddie, I need you to step back."

I do as I'm told. As much as I don't want to, I know I have to. My eyes stay locked on Theo's. His face contorts in pain as the doctor and Matteo roll him onto his side. Doc cuts down the side of his shirt, removing the fabric from his body. "Shouldn't you give him something for the pain," I ask.

"Maddie, it's fine," Theo grits out between his teeth. "You should go and wait for me in the bedroom. I'll be right there."

"Clearly you've lost too much blood if you think for one second I'm leaving this room without you." I fold my arms over my chest.

"It's a clean through and through," the doctor says to no one in particular.

"Thank fuck." Matteo sighs.

"All right. Hold him still," Doc instructs as he picks up a syringe and starts injecting it around the wound.

Half an hour later, I'm in the bathroom with Theo, using a sponge to wash the blood from his body. "If I knew this is all it took to get you to give me a sponge bath, I would have gotten shot weeks ago, bambolina," he says, leaning against the bathroom counter with a pained smirk.

"Not funny. What happened?" I ask him, knowing he probably won't tell me.

He searches my face for a minute. I don't know what he sees but eventually he sighs and says, "The man I shot in the strip club belonged to the Gambino family. I knew it at the time but didn't care. Tonight I had a sit down with their boss. I got jumped in the street on the way to my car."

I've researched the Gambino family. After a man named Harry Gambino came to my parents' funeral, introduced himself, and handed me a card, saying if I ever found myself in any trouble I should call the number printed there. I Google searched the shit out of that name. I then hid the card in a drawer somewhere and never thought of that strange encounter again. "The Gambino family did this to you?" I ask, wondering if that card is still in a drawer in my bedroom.

"No, it was the Russians." Neo walks into the bathroom. Neither of them seem to care that Theo is as naked as the day he was born right now. I, however, do care. I hand Theo a towel.

"Are you sure?" Theo asks.

"Yep, Angelica got one of them. Assholes left him behind."

Huh, guess this mafia thing is a whole family business. I was always under the impression the women were kept at home while the men went and worked. Well, that's how my mom explained it to me anyway. Telling me that girls had no power in the families, and they were sold to whomever provided the best business connection or offer to their fathers. I'm starting to think maybe my mother was a little jaded. I know I shouldn't think that, but I haven't seen any of the men in Theo's family treat women *less than*.

"I'm out. Don't fucking leave this apartment until you hear from me or your father. Also, you should probably call your mother." Neo laughs as Theo groans.

"You told her?" he complains.

"Nope, your Pops did," Neo answers over his shoulder.

"Right." Theo rolls his eyes.

"Come on, I'll help you into bed, then I'll find your phone so you can call your mom."

"I'd much rather you help me into bed and then help my cock find your pussy," he replies with a smirk.

"Yeah, not likely."

"Worth a shot." He shrugs. His hard cock is *hard* to miss when he drops the towel and climbs into bed. I do my best to tamp down my own desires, my need to have him inside me. He's hurt, and I have no doubt the pain meds the doc gave him will kick in quickly *after* I force him to take them.

I t's New Year's Eve. Theo is doing a lot better, although his body is covered in bruises. His phone rings on the bedside table, waking me from my sleep. I see the name *Doc* light up the screen so I answer it. "Hello."

There's a pause before I hear a throat clear. "Ah, Maddie, is it?"

"Yep."

"Is Theo there?" he asks.

"Yeah, hold on. I'll find him." Wrapping a robe around my waist, I walk out of the bedroom and find Theo in the kitchen. He shouldn't be on his feet, yet there he is, cooking a breakfast that could feed an army. "Theo, the doctor is on the phone for you." I hand him his cell.

Theo looks from me to the phone; a strange glint crosses his eyes. "Hello."

I don't wait around to hear what they're talking about. Instead, I head back to the bedroom and straight for the bathroom. After showering, I get dressed and return to the kitchen, where I find Theo and Luca whispering to each other.

"Hey." I let my presence be known and both men look up at me.

"Maddie, good morning." Theo wraps his arms around me and kisses my forehead. "Here, your coffee is ready."

"Thanks. What's going on? Why do you two look like you've been caught with your fingers in the cookie jar?" I ask them.

"Doc found a match for Lilah," Theo says, and I swear the ground under me sways.

"What?"

"Doc... that's why he was calling this morning. He found a match. Lilah is getting that kidney." He smiles.

My eyes water uncontrollably. She's going to get a kidney. She's actually going to get a kidney. "Who?" I ask.

That's when Luca grins. "Me."

I can't keep the shock from my face. Luca is a match. Luca is going to donate a kidney to my sister. "Oh my god, Luca." I wrap my arms around him and then it hits me. He might not feel like he has a choice in this, and as much as I want Lilah to get the new kidney she needs, I don't want someone to be forced to donate one. Stepping back, I wipe at my cheeks. "You don't have to do this. I want you to know that you have a choice here, no matter what Theo says. You can say no. You don't have to give up one of your kidneys for us."

"Maddie, it's fine. I only need one anyway.

Besides, I'm hardly going to let Lilah continue to suffer when I'm able to help her."

"Well, I don't actually know what to say," I tell him.

"You don't have to say anything. We're family, and this is what family does for each other," he replies, leaving the kitchen.

I sit down on one of the stools. I'm in shock. I don't know what to say. I've always dreamed of getting the phone call that said the hospital had a kidney for her. I just... I have no words for how relieved, scared, excited, and unsure I feel right now.

"Are you okay?" Theo asks, standing beside me. He leans his hip on the counter.

"I don't know. I mean, yeah. This is good, right?" I ask him.

"It's fucking fantastic, Maddie. We have a match. She won't have to live her life hooked up to a machine every couple of days anymore."

I nod. "I don't know how to thank you for this, Theo."

"You don't need to. Come on, let's get everyone fed. Trust me when I say you do not want to deal with a hangry Romeo."

I laugh, pushing up from the stool, and help Theo carry platters of food to the table. He's still limping slightly but refuses to not be on his feet.

After breakfast, Theo takes me into his office and locks the door. "I have to ask you something,

Maddie. I don't want to bring you into this, but I don't know what else to do," he says, pacing the room.

"Okay, just ask."

"Did your parents ever mention anything about a locket?" he questions.

"Um, I don't think so, why?"

"Gambino wanted me to find some locket that your father stole from the Russians. Apparently it's the key to keeping the peace, and if the Russians get their hands on it again, war will break out."

"Um, I don't know. They never said anything to me about any locket."

"Okay. Did your mom have a jewelry safe or anything?"

This has me laughing. "We were middle class, Theo. We didn't have jewelry safes. She had a small jewelry box."

"Do you still have it?" he prompts.

"Of course I do. It's in my bedroom."

"Okay, well, I guess it's worth a look. Come on." He takes my hand and opens the door.

"Wait, you're not supposed to leave the apartment," I remind him.

He looks back at me with a smirk. "Bambolina, rules were made to be broken."

An hour later, we're walking up to my apartment. It's only been a few days since I've been here, but for some reason, it seems like a lifetime. Unlocking the door, I walk straight into my bedroom and find my mother's jewelry box, emptying the contents onto my bed. Theo silently picks up each necklace, each little trinket, inspecting them one at a time. None of them are lockets though.

"Show me the box," he says. Handing it over, I watch as he taps his fingers around the interior. Then he throws the whole thing on the ground, causing the wood to splinter and break with the impact.

"What the hell, Theo?" I shriek. But then I see it. A tiny fleck of gold amongst the debris. "What is that?" I ask, picking it up. It's a small locket. I turn it over and read the inscription on the back: *anime unite.* "United souls," I translate the words aloud.

"This is what Old Man Harry was so hung up on finding?" Theo asks, taking the trinket from my hand. He opens it up and peeks at the contents. "Huh," he muses, staring at whatever's inside.

"What is it?" I ask, peering over his shoulder.

"This woman. She looks like you, your mother,

but this photo is too dated to be your mom. It has to be… your grandmother," Theo says.

"My grandmother…?" I knew I had one living grandparent. My mom told me stories about her mother and how she wished we could meet her. But that it wasn't safe. So we never did. I thought about finding her after my parents died. Considered reaching out, but I never did. I couldn't risk Lilah's safety.

"Feel like a family reunion, bambolina?" Theo asks me.

"Not particularly," I murmur. I don't know why, but I don't care to meet my parents' families. They're the reason why we had to be in hiding all those years.

"Okay, you don't have to come, but I do need to pay your grandmother a visit. I can have Matteo escort you back to the apartment," Theo says.

"No, I'm not leaving you." My hand clings to the sleeve of his suit jacket, like that's enough to keep him with me.

Theo's eyebrows draw down. "Maddie, what's wrong?"

"Please, just take me with you. I don't want to not be with you." My voice trembles.

"Okay, I'll take you with me."

Once we're in the back of the car again, with his brother driving and Theo seated next to me, he turns and looks at me. My hand is gripping his so tight my knuckles are white. "Bambolina, what's going on?"

"I'm scared," I admit.

"I'm not going to let anything happen to you." He leans in and peppers the top of my head with kisses.

"I'm scared of something happening to you," I clarify. I'm not scared for myself. I'm scared of letting him out of my sight again.

"I'm fine. I'm right here. I'm not going anywhere." He picks up our joined hands and kisses my knuckles. "I mean, could you really see Matteo taking on the role of boss when Pops retires?" Theo laughs.

"Hey, I can hear you, asshole," Matteo grumbles from the front of the car.

"I don't care," Theo shoots back.

When we pull up to a gated estate, Matteo rolls down his window. "Here to see Mrs. Mortello." The gates open and the car proceeds up the long driveway. Theo keeps my hand firmly in his as we exit the vehicle and walk up the front stairs. As soon as the doors open, we're quickly led into a sitting room.

"Mrs. Mortello, it's good to see you," Theo says. "This is my girlfriend, Maddie."

The old woman stands and hugs me. "It's a pleasure to meet you, Maddie." Stepping back with unshed tears in her eyes, she whispers, "You look so much like her."

"It's nice to meet you."

"Come, sit. Do you want a drink? Tea? coffee?"

Theo looks to me and I shake my head. "No, we're good."

We sit on a love seat opposite the older woman, who I understand to be my grandmother. It's strange. I know *technically* she's my family, but I feel nothing for her.

"We came to ask if you knew anything about this, Mrs. Mortello?" Theo hands her the locket.

She gasps. "Where did you find this?"

"It was in my mother's jewelry box," I tell her.

"This was mine," she says, staring at the tiny locket.

"Any idea why Harry Gambino would want it?" Theo questions, straight to the point.

"Yes, I know exactly why." She sighs. "He's trying to protect me." Then she looks me directly in the eye. "And he's trying to protect you and your sister."

"Why?" I ask, though I should be asking if she knew about me and Lilah, then why has she never come for us?

"We were young, foolish, and in love," she

explains with a faraway look in her eyes. "Our affair was supposed to stop after I got married. But we couldn't. We didn't." Suddenly pushing to her feet, she walks over to the mantle and picks up a frame with a photo of my mother in it—a photo from her youth, long before my sister and I were born. "Lana wasn't my husband's child. She was Harry's," she admits.

"What?" Theo asks. "That's why Gambino wants this locket, to keep your nasty fucking affair a secret?"

"You don't understand... if the Mortellos or the Gambinos found out about this, it would mean devastation like no other. It's the biggest betrayal, what we did, what *I* did. They will kill all of us. Including the girls."

"That's why my parents ran, isn't it? Someone found out?" I press her.

"The Petrovs weren't as thrilled with your father marrying Lana as they pretended to be. But the Gambino family is worth billions, in oils and stocks. Somehow Nikolai Petrov discovered the truth. He was blackmailing Harry with the information, but the only way he could prove his theory was by using your mother's DNA. No respectful Italian would ever believe his word without proof." She sits back down before continuing. "Your father heard what his brother was planning and ran. He took Lana and was just gone."

"What's so important about the locket then? It doesn't prove shit." Theo's brows draw down as he tries to piece everything together.

"The locket itself—no, it doesn't. I don't know why Harry wants this back. But you and Lilah, you girls are the proof." Mrs. Mortello looks to me.

I don't get it… My mother and father were in hiding for twenty years, all to protect a secret affair my grandmother had. I'm so angry right now. How could people be so damn selfish? "Theo, I need you to take me home," I say, standing. I don't bother saying goodbye to the older woman as I walk out of her house. I have no intention of ever returning.

CHAPTER 26

Theo

I leave Maddie sleeping in bed and head to my office. Picking up my phone, I call Harry Gambino. "Valentino," he answers.

"I found your locket."

"Great. I knew you would. Where is it?" he asks.

"I left it with Mrs. Mortello. She's the rightful owner of it after all, isn't she?" I counter.

"She told you?" He sighs.

"I'm going to tell you this once. If anyone finds out about your sordid affairs, Maddie and Lilah are not part of it. If anyone comes for them, I will hold you and your family accountable."

"Those two girls are set to inherit the Gambino fortune when I die, Theo," he says.

"Change your fucking will then, old man, and do it soon. Neither Maddie nor Lilah will ever need a dime from you. Like I said, they're Valentinos now." I hang up. I probably should have discussed it with Maddie first, before telling him they didn't want what was rightfully theirs to inherit. But fuck that, I'll take it to my fucking grave. She's family now. My family.

I toss the phone aside and walk to the wall, pulling the painting away and unlocking the safe. Reaching in, I pick up the little black velvet box I set there and open the lid. I personally designed the stone that sits cushioned inside. Three carats, princess cut. Because Maddie is a fucking princess and deserves nothing but the best. Placing the box in my pocket, I head into the kitchen and start breakfast. It's going to be a long fucking day. It's New Year's Eve, and we're expected at my uncle's estate in just five hours. My plans were to propose to Maddie at midnight in front of our whole family. But I'm getting fucking impatient and want to see this ring on her finger as soon as possible.

I make quick work of cooking up some pancakes, coffee, and juice. Positioning everything on a cart, I place the sterling silver dome-shaped plate covers over the food to keep it warm before taking it all up to the rooftop. I set up the little two-seater table, then I head back into the apartment and straight for my girl. Leaning over her sleeping form, I tuck her hair away from her cheek. "Bambolina, it's time to wake up." I pepper her face with kisses.

Her hand swats out and pushes me aside. "Just a

few more minutes. I'm not ready," she grumbles, her voice husky with sleep.

My dick stirs in my pants. I do my best to tamp down my desire. *Hard* is a constant fucking state when it comes to Maddie. "Come on, Maddie, I've got breakfast and coffee." I pull the blankets off her, holding out her robe for her to take.

She peeks one eye open at me. "Why do you look like that?" she asks, pointing a finger and waving it over the length of me.

"Like what?"

"Why are you wearing a suit already?" She pops up and takes the robe.

"We have a busy day. I wanted to get an early start. Come on." I take her hand and pick up the throw blanket from the end of the bed.

Once I've led Maddie into the elevator, she throws me a curious look. "Where are you taking me? I thought you said you had coffee."

"I do." The doors open to the rooftop and we step out. The air is chilly and snow covers the ground. I turn on the outdoor heater positioned beside the table. "Come, sit." I pull a chair out and wrap the blanket around Maddie.

"Thank you. It's beautiful up here, Theo." Her voice is full of awe as she scans her surroundings.

"It is," I say, my gaze locked on hers. I take a huge breath in and my hands shake as I remove the lid to her plate. I don't think I've ever been this fucking nervous in my life.

Maddie glances down at the plate, up to me, then back to the plate. She sits there with wide eyes, silently staring at the stack of pancakes topped with maple syrup, ice cream, and a three-carat diamond ring. Kneeling down next to her, I take her hands in mine. I've rehearsed what I wanted to say to her a million times. But as I sit here—the cold, wet snow going straight through my knee and down to my toes —it all goes out the window.

"Maddie, I never thought I would find you. I never thought I was deserving of something as good as you are. I'm not deserving. But I don't care. I want to keep you. Will you let me keep you, Maddie? Forever? Will you marry me?" I ask her. Tears drip down her cheeks. I reach a hand up and wipe them away. I should remind her that she promised to say yes to every question I ask her today. That was her Christmas gift to me.

"Y-yes," she says, surprising the hell out of me.

"Yes?" I parrot the word, needing to hear her say it again.

"Yes," she responds more confidently.

"Thank fuck. I really didn't want to have to kidnap you and lock you away in a tower forever if you said no." I laugh, but it's not a joke. I was fully prepared to do just that. I pick up the ring and slide it onto her hand. "I promise I will do everything I can to give you the life you deserve, Maddie, to be the kind of husband who is worthy of you." I pop her finger in my mouth and suck and lick it clean.

"Theo, you are worthy of me. You deserve everything good in life. You are a good person." She slams her lips onto mine, wrapping her arms around my neck as she jumps onto me. I fall backwards, with Maddie sprawled out on top of me.

"Mmm, you have made me the happiest man alive," I tell her between kisses.

In the elevator heading back down to the apartment after we've finished eating, I press the stop button and cage Maddie up against the wall. "So, how about tomorrow?" I ask.

"What about tomorrow?" Her eyebrows draw down.

"Getting married. What do you think about tomorrow? I mean, it's New Year's Day. I'd never be at risk of forgetting our anniversary. Not that I could ever forget the day you legally became mine." I raise my eyebrows.

Maddie laughs. "You're crazy. No, we're not getting married tomorrow. I mean, if you're dead set on getting married on New Year's Day, then we can do twelve months from now."

"Now you're the one who's crazy, if you think I'm waiting twelve months to marry you." I press the button on the lift.

As we enter the apartment, we are met by utter chaos. Romeo and Luca are brawling on the floor of the living room. Lilah is standing off to the side with a look of complete shock—and, oh fuck, are those tears? They fucking are.

I drop Maddie's hand. "Matteo! Get your ass out here now!" I yell as I make hasty steps towards my idiot brothers. Grabbing Romeo by the back of his shirt, I pull him off his twin. It's not unusual for us to fight with each other. What *is* unusual is the ferocity of their exchanged blows. But their brotherly issues are not my concern right now. "Who the fuck made her cry?" I gesture to Lilah. It's at this point that Matteo decides to make an appearance.

"What's going on?" he asks.

"Where were you while these two fucking heathens were destroying my fucking living room?" I ask him. "And I'm still waiting for an answer from *you*?" I turn back to the twins.

"Uh, Theo, I'm fine. Really, it wasn't them," Lilah says.

"Then why are you crying?" I deadpan.

"Um, I may have overheard Luca tell Romeo

about the kidney thing… that he's going to give me a kidney," she says in the quietest voice.

I turn back to my brothers. "My office, now!" I shove at Romeo's back, pushing him down the hall. This conversation does not need to be had in front of Lilah or Maddie. I don't know what their fucking issue is. But I'll be sure to put an end to it. I wait for them to be out of sight before I turn back to Lilah. "Are you sure those idiots didn't say or do anything?" I ask her.

"I'm sure. I'm fine. Really, I didn't mean to cause any drama. I promise," she says.

"You haven't."

The doors to the elevator open with a ping, and I groan. There are only so many people who have access to this penthouse and most of them are already fucking in it. Pivoting on my heel, I'm greeted by a glare from my father as my mother rushes towards me. I grunt when she wraps her arms around me. I may have split a stitch open when Maddie jumped on me earlier. I haven't looked, but if the warm trickling sensation is any indication, it's safe to say I have. Thank God for black clothing—the color is forgiving when it comes to spilled blood.

"Oh my god, Theo, are you okay? What the hell happened? Why aren't you in bed? You should be resting," my mother scolds, and her tone has me almost wanting to hop back into bed and follow her orders.

"I'm fine, Ma. Promise. Takes more than a little bullet to keep me down." I kiss her cheek. Whispering in her ear, I say, "She said yes."

The shriek that leaves my mother's mouth deafens me. But it works. She forgets all about me and spins on her heel to face Maddie. "Oh my gosh, I have a daughter. T, we have a daughter," she says to Dad before engulfing Maddie in an airtight hug. "I'm so excited, Maddie. Show me the ring." Mom doesn't wait for Maddie to lift her hand. Instead, she takes hold of her left arm and holds it up. "Oh, it's so beautiful."

"Thank you," Maddie says shyly.

"What happened out here?" Pops asks, nodding at the fallen lamps, broken glass, and sofa now on its back.

"Your delinquent children happened—that's what. The twins are waiting in the office. I'm about to go in there and kick both of their asses, so if either of you..." I point to my parents. "...have any final words for your good-for-nothing offspring, best be voicing them now before I fucking kill them," I growl.

"Theo. Language! And you're not killing your brothers. Stop being dramatic. T, go and sort out your children. Maddie, Lilah, and I are going to make mimosas and start planning the wedding of the century!" Mom doesn't give anyone an option when it comes to her plans, as she takes each of the girls' hands in one of hers and leads them off in the direction of the kitchen.

"I hope you realize you've created a monster. Your mother has been planning each of your weddings since before you were even born." Pops smirks.

"Good, means I won't have much to do other than turn up." I shrug, making my way into the office. It's my father who slams the door shut. Romeo and Luca both pale when they notice he's here.

Good, fuckers, I hope your scared.

"Pops, I didn't know you were coming in today," Luca says.

"Clearly," he replies. Heading over to the wet bar, he pours himself a drink. "Care to explain why your brother's home looks like a hurricane ran through it?"

The twins look at each other. "We just had a minor disagreement. It's nothing. Water under the bridge," Romeo grits between clenched teeth. Whatever it is, it's obviously not that simple.

"You're brothers. You're on the same fucking team. We have enough people trying to kill us without killing each other. Whatever *this* is, sort it out. And whatever Theo has to replace out there." He points in the direction of the living room. "...it's coming out of your allowances."

At this, I smirk. I like expensive shit. I know how much my brothers get, and usually, replacing a few broken vases and lamps wouldn't make much of a fucking dent. But the ones I'll be replacing them with —yeah, I'll make sure it hurts their pockets.

"What? Pops, that's not fair."

"What's not fair is that your brother took a beating and a fucking bullet for your asses and then you come here and destroy his home."

The twins look to me, and if I thought they were pale before, they're sheet-white now.

"What are you talking about? What do they have to do with the Russians who jumped me?" I ask, leaning against the bookshelf. I casually cross one leg in front of the other, keeping my hands in my pockets so I don't accidently choke the life out of one or both of them.

"That's what I'm here to find out," Pops says, taking a seat on one of the sofas. "Start talking," he directs this to Romeo and Luca.

Matteo, who has been silent this whole time, curses under his breath while helping himself to my fucking whiskey before coming to stand next to me— clearly showing where his loyalty lies. Don't get me wrong: he's not ever going to let me kill those boys, not that I actually would, but he'll help me make them hurt if they deserve it.

"It wasn't our fault." This comes from Luca.

"It never fucking is," I grunt.

"He fucking deserved it. He hurt her in the worst way, so we put him in the hospital," Romeo says.

"Who did you put in the hospital and who did they hurt?" Our father is clearly getting agitated at the lack of explanation.

"Livvy... That fucker attacked her. He...." Romeo trails off, his face appearing tortured, hurt, angry.

"He hurt her, so we hurt him. Stephan Petrov. He deserved it, Pops, swear it," Luca says.

"Who is this Livvy?" Pops asks Romeo, ignoring Luca.

"She's, ah, my tutor," Romeo says.

"Romeo, you're trying my last nerve here, son. You have a fucking 4.0 GPA. Why the fuck do you need a tutor?"

"I... I'm not sure. But she is, and I wasn't going to stand by and let that fucker get away with hurting her," Romeo hisses.

"Right," Pops says.

I look at my brother. It's written all over his face. He's in love with this Livvy girl. And honestly, I can't fucking hold it against him. I would have done the same thing. "It's fine, Pops. What's the plan from here?" I say.

"It's done. Eye for an eye and all that bullshit. We hospitalized one of theirs; they put a bullet through one of ours." He shrugs, then adds, "The Petrovs know nothing about those girls. And we need to fucking keep it that way."

"Agreed," all four of us say in unison.

Epilogue

MADDIE

THREE MONTHS LATER

I never thought I could be this happy. This settled and content. But here I am.

As I look around at the familiar faces, the faces of the women I both admire and love, I know I couldn't have asked for a better life right now. She would have loved this—my mom. I wish more than anything that she could be here. A little peace settles over me knowing that she's more than likely watching over me in this moment.

Standing in the middle of the bridal store, I take in all the open-mouthed, wide-eyed stares, but it's Theo's mother who comes up to me first. Wrapping me in her arms, she whispers, "I'm sure your mother is smiling down on you today, Maddie. You look absolutely stunning."

"Thank you," I say, trying and failing to keep the tears at bay. I glance over at Savannah, my soon-to-be sister in-law—well, that's if Matteo can keep her without fucking it up. Then I look to Gia and Lilah, and I can't help the goofy smile spreading across my face. "Great, I'm done. It's your turn now. Bridesmaid dresses, here we come."

Savannah and Lilah groan, but Gia jumps up and down on the spot. "Yes! I've been training my whole life for this moment."

I laugh at my best friend's antics, but she's not wrong. We have been training our whole lives—the number of times we would dress up in our mothers' heels and dresses is actually a little embarrassing. "You take that section with Savannah. Lilah, I need your help getting out of this thing." I drag my sister into the dressing room. As soon as the door is shut, I ask her, "How are you feeling?"

"For the millionth time today, I'm fine. Stop worrying." She starts to unbutton the back of my gown.

"I can't help but worry," I tell her. She just got out of the hospital a week ago. Her transplant seems to be taking well but anything could happen. The immunosuppressants could stop working, infection could spread, the organ could fail... I take a breath to stop my mind from reeling.

I will be forever thankful to Luca for what he did. It's not easy to just give up a body part, and he did it without thought. He wanted to do the surgery right away, as soon as we found out he was a match. But Lilah refused, saying she wanted to wait until the end of his football season. She didn't want to take away his life just to save hers. He argued, insisting that football would still be there next year. Although, considering the fact that his team was in the playoffs and won the championship, I guess it's a good thing she made him wait. Winning a championship isn't something that you can experience all that often in your lifetime, I'm sure.

The surgery was all set for February, then Lilah got sick with pneumonia and was hospitalized for a few weeks. We had to reschedule. She finally received that much-needed kidney in March. And here we are, a few weeks later, moving on with our lives while planning my wedding to the most amazing man I've ever met.

"You don't know how much it means to me that you're here. That you're getting better, Lilah. I didn't... I never want to do this life without you," I tell her.

"I know." She nods silently. "Maddie?" she questions.

"Yeah?"

"What's going to happen after the wedding? I mean, with me? Are you and Theo going to want me to, like, move out? You'll be starting your own family, and I don't want to be a burden to you anymore."

I stop her rambling. "Hold that thought," I tell her. Pulling out my phone, I dial Theo and put him on speaker phone.

"Bambolina, aren't you supposed to be shopping for a certain white dress right now?" he answers.

"Yep, I'm in the changing room with Lilah. She asked me a question that I thought you might be better at answering." I smile.

"Okay," he says, though skeptically.

"She wants to know if she has to move out after we get married." I know my sister means well, but anticipating what's about to come out of Theo's mouth has me fighting back a laugh.

"What the actual fuck? Move out? Is she fucking crazy, Maddie? She's a child. Where the fuck does she think she's going? Fuck me, tell her she can move out when she's like thirty. Actually, scratch that. She can move out over my dead fucking body." He curses, and I can hear his footsteps as he clearly paces up and down.

"Yeah, that's what I thought." I chuckle to myself. "Thanks, Theo, gotta go. I love you."

"I love you too. Make sure she knows she's not allowed to move out," he says before cutting the call.

"Does that answer your question?" I grin.

"Uh-huh, sure. But... he does know I'm going to be starting college in August, right?" She raises an eyebrow.

"Um, yeah, I haven't told him about that yet." I laugh, knowing he's going to hate it. But I'm so proud of Lilah. She's managed to not only keep up with her studies but get ahead, and was even accepted for early admissions into her college of choice. *A whole year early.*

Maybe he'll find some peace in the knowledge that she'll be attending college with his brothers. The twins are fiercely protective of my sister. I don't think anything could possibly happen to her with those boys around.

About the Author

kylie kent
SEXY, ALWAYS AND FOREVER ROMANCE

Kylie made the leap from kindergarten teacher to romance author, living out her dream to deliver sexy, always and forever romances. She loves a happily ever after story with tons of built-in steam.

She currently resides in Perth, Australia and when she is not dreaming up the latest romance, she can be found spending time with her three children and her husband of twenty years, her very own real-life instant-love.

Kylie loves to hear from her readers; you can reach her at: author.kylie.kent@gmail.com

Printed in Great Britain
by Amazon